Leesa had known she was lying to herself.

She had applied for the research fellowship to be near Hamish again. He hadn't completely broken her heart two years previously with his unpassionate revelations—just sprained it a little. Leesa realised she might as well stop breathing before she would ever manage to succeed in controlling her emotions. Hamish O'Donnell was the man for her. Her soul mate.

Now all she had to do…was convince him.

Lucy Clark began writing romance in her early teens and immediately knew she'd found her 'calling' in life. After working as a secretary in a busy teaching hospital, she turned her hand to writing medical romance. She currently lives in Adelaide, Australia, and has the desire to travel the world with her husband. Lucy largely credits her writing success to the support of her husband, family and friends.

Recent titles by the same author:

PARTNERS FOR LIFE
MOTHER TO BE
POTENTIAL HUSBAND

PARTNERS
FOR EVER

BY
LUCY CLARK

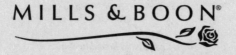

MILLS & BOON®

To Lizanne and Graham.
Thanks for your support!
Pr 27:10

*First published in Great Britain 2000
Harlequin Mills & Boon Limited,
Eton House, 18-24 Paradise Road, Richmond, Surrey TW9 1SR*

© Lucy Clark 2000

ISBN 0 263 82269 9

*Set in Times Roman 10½ on 11¼ pt.
03-0011-50732*

*Printed and bound in Spain
by Litografia Rosés, S.A., Barcelona*

CHAPTER ONE

'DO YOU take this woman to be your lawfully wedded wife?'

Leesa slowly transferred her gaze from the minister to Hamish. He was her one true love. Her heart hammered in her chest when she realised he was looking back at her. She blinked quickly with embarrassment, before giving him a shy smile.

The midnight blue of his eyes intensified and for a brief moment Leesa could have sworn she saw a flash of desire but it was quickly veiled. Now was not the time or the place.

'To have and to hold...'

Leesa focused on the minister's words. She would dearly love to have *and* hold Hamish.

'For better, for worse...'

Nothing could be worse than her life without Hamish. Together, she knew they would conquer any challenges that came their way.

'For richer, for poorer...'

Money had never meant that much to her anyway. Her entire upbringing had been based on the fact that if she had what she needed, the rest was a bonus—and at the moment all she *needed* was Hamish.

'In sickness and in health...'

Well, the fact that they were both qualified doctors would assist her in keeping that end of the bargain.

'To love and to cherish...'

That would *never* be a problem. She had loved and cherished Hamish for years already.

'Until you are parted by death?'

Leesa refused to even consider Hamish's death. The thought brought tears to her eyes, a lump to her throat and an agonising pain to her heart.

The minister had finished speaking. She waited, the minister waited, the entire congregation made up of family and friends waited.

'I will,' the groom said clearly, and smiled at his bride.

Leesa sighed wistfully at her sister Janet's shimmering gown of white, fervently wishing they could change places. Although, if that happened, she would end up marrying Angus, Hamish's younger brother, with whom her older sister was deeply in love.

The similarities between the brothers were very strong. They both sported jet black hair and the O'Donnell family's famous blue eyes. Hamish's, though, were darker, more intense than those of his sibling.

The two families had known each other for years—ever since Leesa had been teenager—and seven months ago Angus had returned to their home town of Newcastle after eight years of travelling the globe. He'd been working, not only as a general practitioner in six-monthly locum positions but also as a super-sleuth for a pharmaceutical company. Janet's own general practice had begun to expand and Angus had returned, creating havoc with her sister's emotions from the very beginning.

When they'd announced their engagement, both families had been ecstatic. Especially Leesa, as it meant further opportunities to be with Hamish. Even though they worked together, he the orthopaedic consultant and she the orthopaedic registrar, the only 'social' time they shared was either studying or at family gatherings. In the past few years, because both sets of parents worked overseas, those family gatherings had been few and far between.

She knew Hamish still saw her as the thirteen-year-old schoolgirl she'd been when they'd initially met, but that had been sixteen years ago. Leesa was now twenty-nine, yet Hamish still looked upon her as the kid sister he'd never had.

It was his own fault, Leesa rationalised, that she was completely infatuated with him. He had set the standard for every male she'd ever dated and none of them had measured up. Hamish was charming, witty and adorably sexy. He managed to get her pulse racing with a single look and Leesa knew she was a lost cause.

During medical school he'd tutored her, helping her study for final exams. After she'd graduated, he'd recommended her for internship.

Hamish had urged her to further her mind, always encouraging her to take that extra step, go that extra mile, and because of his commitment and insistence Leesa had graduated at the top of her class. The dux.

But still…throughout all her accomplishments Hamish only looked upon her as a sister. The flash of desire she'd thought she'd seen in his eyes only moments ago had been the product of her imagination. There was no way he would find her desirable. In his mind, they were *family*.

The friendship he offered meant more to her than gold. If that was all she could get from him, she would accept it—for now. But one day…one day his eyes would be opened and he would see her, not as a gauche teenager but as a nearly qualified orthopaedic surgeon who was a mature woman.

'You may now kiss your bride,' the minister announced, and a round of applause swept through the church. Leesa scolded herself. Once again, her thoughts had been lost in 'Hamish land' and she'd missed the end of Janet's vows.

Soon Mr and Mrs Angus O'Donnell were walking out of the church, stopping here and there in the aisle to receive congratulations from various friends and relations. Leesa's arm was snug in the crook of Hamish's elbow as they slowly followed the newlyweds out—and she enjoyed every moment of being so close to him.

A few hours later, Leesa sat down in the corner of the reception room and kicked off her shoes. Almost everyone else was up dancing, enjoying themselves, as was expected at a wedding reception. Leesa looked across to Janet who was laughing at her new husband, happier than she'd ever been.

Leesa pulled the ankle-length, deep-red, velvet dress up so she could rest her ankle on her knee to begin massaging her foot. She closed her eyes in momentary relief before a deep male voice whispered close to her ear, 'That's not very ladylike, Leesa.'

Her eyes snapped open and she looked up into Hamish's smiling face. She returned his smile and shrugged.

'Since when have I *ever* been ladylike?'

'True,' he agreed on a laugh, and sat down beside her.

'You weren't supposed to agree,' she muttered, but kept on massaging.

'Would you like another drink?'

'No, thanks.'

'Are you sure? After all, it is the groomsman's job to take care of the bridesmaid.'

'I'm fine.' Leesa's pulse rate increased for a moment. She could give him some tips on how best to take care of her—and she knew they'd shock him.

'But your feet aren't fine.' Hamish shook his head. 'You're just not used to wearing three inch heels, are you, Leesa?'

'I'm not used to wearing *any* heels. You know I wear flats to work and running shoes at all other times.'

'Yes, I do,' he replied with a nod. 'I must say, though…' Hamish stopped her hands and gently lifted her ankle, resting it on his thigh before he took over the massage '…that the heels, combined with the long split at the back of your dress, reveal a generous amount of those luscious legs you keep hidden under trousers day in, day out.'

Leesa's pulse rate shot to boiling point. His massaging

fingers suddenly took on a sensual feel. Tingles flooded her body and she was thankful to be sitting. Allowing his words to sink in, Leesa frowned then shook her head, not entirely sure she'd heard him correctly. 'Did you…did you just pay me a compliment?' Her voice was a little breathless but under the circumstances…

'No.' He burst her bubble. 'I was merely stating the facts. You have great legs.' He shrugged as though there was nothing else to it. His thumbs continued to ease the pain in her foot while his words left her emotions high in the air and even more confused than before.

Hamish thought she had great legs. This was a start, she realised. Even though the revelation had been given without commitment, it was definitely a beginning.

Feeling empowered as never before, Leesa decided to press things a little further.

'So…what else…do you think is…great…about me?' Her mouth had gone dry and she ran her tongue over her lips. She adored him when he was all playful like this. The excitement within her grew, and with it her boldness. Perhaps tonight they might be able to get a few things straight. For instance—the fact that Leesa wasn't a little girl any more and more than capable of playing adult games with Hamish.

'Fishing?' Hamish laughed, but nodded. 'All right. I'll play. Apart from the obvious, being that you're an extremely smart and intelligent girl…'

She ignored the 'girl' part, giving him her undivided attention, eager to hear what he would say.

'You have great feet.'

'Feet?' she queried, falling rather flat at his answer.

'Yes.' He placed her foot on the floor and picked up the other one.

'Until tonight,' Leesa pointed out, as his thumbs began the rhythmic rubbing over her aching foot, 'I doubt if you've ever *seen* my feet.'

Hamish thought for a moment. 'You're correct.' He was silent for some time, before saying, 'It's hardly your feet that keep me awake at night.'

'Pardon?' Leesa wasn't sure she'd heard him correctly. Hamish? Being kept awake—over *her?* When he didn't reply she asked, 'How much have you had to drink?'

'Probably too much if you need to ask that question.' He continued to massage and said matter-of-factly, 'Leesa, you are a beautiful and desirable woman. Your body is next to perfect, your neck begs to be nuzzled, your blue eyes make a man drown whenever he looks into them, your hair shines like spun gold and your lips were made to be kissed.'

Although his words were everything Leesa had ever wanted to hear, they were all said calmly, with no feeling. No *passion.*

'What *I* think is beside the point, however,' he went on. 'You're *family.* My desire for you has no place in the rational scheme of things and I've come to accept that. I've watched you grow and mature into the most stunning of your sex, but you're like a sister to me and I would never do anything to hurt you.'

'Y-you…just can't…' she faltered, trying desperately to get a hold on herself, forcing back the tears that threatened to spill over. 'Hamish, why have you never…?' She stopped, a surge of anger spreading throughout her body. '*Sister?* That's it?' She tried again. 'How can you say all those things—words I've been…dreaming of hearing—without the slightest hint of emotion?'

'Leesa.' His tone was indulgent as he placed her foot to the ground and took her hand. 'All I'm telling you are the facts. I call them as I see them.' He gave her a winning smile, and she realised he was trying to soften the blow. 'I know you're infatuated with me but it's, well, it's irrelevant.'

'*Irrelevant!*' She snatched her hand back from his. 'Irrelevant,' she repeated, her voice a disgusted, choked whisper. 'What's irrelevant, Hamish, is your inability to let your soul be touched. All these years you've been my mentor. You've guided me, taught me and urged me to better myself and not once, not *once* have you allowed your heart to feel. To exult in my triumphs—or your own for that matter.

'I'd be surprised if you even *understood* what's happened here today—the way your brother and my sister have been joined together through love. *Love,* Hamish. It's obviously something you know nothing about, and if you continue in this manner you never will.'

'Leesa,' he tried to reason, 'aren't you overreacting?'

'How would you know, Hamish? You refuse to allow yourself to even *admit* you *have* a heart.' She rose to her feet, struggling valiantly to keep control of her emotions. 'I guess I should thank you. You've allowed me to see the *real* Hamish O'Donnell at long last.'

Leesa looked down at the man who had stolen her heart all those years ago. 'You're just a shell, Hamish,' she whispered, her voice full of regret, tears glistening in her eyes. 'The saddest part is you could be *so much more* if you would allow yourself to become a mere mortal—like the rest of us.'

Feeling the tears begin to slide down her cheeks, Leesa ran out of the room, through the hotel lobby and into a taxi that was waiting out front.

As she was driven through the darkened streets of Newcastle, her feet bare, her shoes left behind at the reception room, Leesa allowed the tears to flow down her cheeks and her heart to break.

'Clamp,' Hamish ordered, and waited for the instrument to be placed in his hand. 'Leesa, just move the retractor a little to the right so I can get this artery clamped.' They had almost finished performing a revision total hip replacement on Mr Lewis.

He'd been admitted to Casualty earlier that morning after

slipping on his bathroom floor and landing hard on his right hip, dislocating his right shoulder in the process. Mr Lewis's right hip had been replaced two years ago but the artificial prosthesis had been broken during his fall.

Thankfully for Mr Lewis, there had been a cancellation on Hamish's list and, apart from a quick knee arthroscopy which Leesa had performed in theatre one, her first day on the job was progressing without a hitch.

Leesa moved the retractor as asked and soon the offending artery was no longer causing a problem.

'Good work,' Hamish praised his team. 'How does Mr Lewis's blood pressure look now, Allan?'

'Rising...slowly but improving,' Allan, the anaesthetist, informed him a few moments later.

'Right. I'll just start tidying things up and then I'm ready to begin closing. Are the X-rays of the scapula developed yet?'

'They should be here any moment, Mr O'Donnell,' Theatre Sister announced, and at that moment the scout nurse came in and hooked the radiographs onto the viewer.

'I can manage here, Leesa. Take a look at those films.'

'Whatever you say, boss,' Leesa joked, and smiled at him from behind her mask. Theatre Sister took the retractor from her and with her hands held up, Leesa reviewed the X-rays of Mr Lewis's shoulder.

'There's no sign of fracture and the dislocation looks routine. Do you want me to rotate it back in now?'

'It was once assumed,' Hamish remarked to Theatre Sister, but knew the entire staff was listening, 'that orthopaedic surgery was too difficult for women because it sometimes required brute strength to perform particular procedures—such as relocating bones. Now, I'm not suggesting that Dr Stevenson here is a brute of any kind— quite the opposite.' He raised his eyebrows suggestively above his mask and Leesa turned away from him to gaze unseeingly back at the X-rays. Hamish always managed to turn her insides to mush with just a look—and now was no exception.

'But it is a common fact of nature that men are stronger than women,' he continued. 'Yet, lo and behold, our esteemed female orthopods have proven over the years that with a bit of lateral thinking and ingenuity anything can be accomplished.'

Leesa glanced over her shoulder. 'You are a bit long-winded at times, Hamish. Is that a yes or a no?'

She could tell he was smiling beneath his mask and involuntarily smiled back, still waiting for his reply.

'You may proceed, Dr Stevenson,' he assented.

Leesa walked over to the scrub sink, where a nurse helped her de-gown, scrub and re-gown. Hamish had finished his 'tidying-up' and was ready to close. He came over to watch what Leesa was doing, and once the humerus had been neatly relocated into the socket of the scapula he resumed his position and began suturing the wound closed.

'Oh, Dr Stevenson is a *fine* orthopaedic surgeon,' he told the theatre sister. 'I taught her everything she knows.'

'I was wondering about that,' Theatre Sister said. 'After all, Mr O'Donnell, this is Dr Stevenson's first operating procedure as your new research fellow yet you seem completely at ease with each other.'

'Strange,' Hamish remarked with a frown as Leesa returned to stand opposite him, ready to assist in the long but meticulous procedure of closing the wound in layers. 'I would have thought the hospital grapevine abuzz with the story of our lives. Then again, perhaps it's old news.'

'Even if it were, I wouldn't know,' Theatre Sister informed him. 'I never listen to gossip, Mr O'Donnell.'

'*Touché!*' Hamish nodded as he secured the new strand of double zero Vicryl suture between the locking scissors. 'Shall you enlighten her or shall I?' he asked Leesa.

'You're the boss, boss,' Leesa deferred, curious as to how he would explain their relationship.

'Although Dr Stevenson has passed her final orthopaedic exams with flying colours, thereby technically making her a "Mr", and although she has accepted the position as my research fellow for the next twelve months, she's no stranger to this hospital.'

'I did my medical training, internship, service rotation and the beginning of my orthopaedic rotation here,' she informed the sister. 'You've only been here for one year, haven't you?'

'Yes.'

'Then that's why we've never met.'

'I thought you said I could tell the story.' He looked up briefly from his work and frowned at her.

'So I did. We're all captivated. Please, continue.'

'Not only do I know her in a professional sense but also a personal one.'

'I see,' Theatre Sister acknowledged meaningfully, her eyes sparkling with amusement.

'I don't think you do, Sister. Leesa has always been my surrogate sister. I've known her since she was a teenager. Our parents have been close friends as well as colleagues for two decades, and exactly two years ago today my younger brother and Leesa's sister tied the knot.

'So perhaps the reason why there is little or no gossip on the grapevine is because, as far as everyone is concerned, we're viewed as brother and sister.'

And never the twain shall meet, Leesa added silently to herself. Two years today since Hamish had quashed all her hopes of him *ever* seeing her as anything other than a sister. He'd found her attractive in a benign way but after all she was just...Leesa. Still not surprised at the bitterness the memory evoked, she tried to push it to the back of her mind—again!

'Where did you complete your training?' Theatre Sister asked as the final suture layer was completed.

Hamish's spiel had left a sour taste in Leesa's mouth and

she had to clear her throat before answering. 'I did one year in England and last year I was at the children's hospital in Sydney.'

'Ah, so "big brother" here got you the job as his research fellow.'

'He did nothing of the kind,' Leesa responded quickly, a note of defensiveness in her tone.

'Quite true,' Hamish agreed. 'Leesa has remarkable credentials—dux of her graduating year, excellent scientific papers and she even equalled my score in the final orthopaedic exams. Therefore she was the most accomplished applicant I received. During this year, Leesa will also be completing her Ph.D.'

'You sound very proud of her.'

'I am. Although I do take *some* credit for her achievements.'

'You flatter yourself, Hamish,' Leesa interjected.

'Indeed I do.' He laughed. 'I feel that, had I not been there to guide her over the years, Leesa might not have succeeded as well as she has.'

Theatre Sister's eyes met Leesa's as Hamish concentrated on stapling the skin closed. Leesa saw compassion there and her heart lifted in the knowledge that the new theatre sister—whose name she didn't even know yet—understood the giant ego of the surgeon before them.

'Finished,' Hamish announced, and nodded to Allan to begin reversing the anaesthetic. 'Thank you all. Leesa, if you'll finish up here, I'll get the clinic started so we don't run overtime. Bring Mr Lewis's casenotes with you when you come and I'll write them up then.'

With that, Hamish de-gowned and left Theatre.

'And that, as they say, is that,' Theatre Sister said.

'He's not *really* that bad.' Leesa felt inclined to defend him.

'Handsome he may be, but he's also an arrogant, overbearing male who's taking credit for *your* achievements,'

Theatre Sister replied as they began the swab count. When everything was taken care of, Mr Lewis was wheeled out of Theatre and into Recovery, signalling the end of Mr O'Donnell's theatre list.

Theatre Sister accompanied Leesa to the changing rooms.

'Caroline Metcalfe.' She held out her hand, before starting to change out of her theatre garb. 'Sorry we weren't introduced earlier.'

'It was a bit hard as I came into Theatre after Mr Lewis's operation had already begun. I was held up in theatre one with the previous case.'

'Mr. O'Donnell couldn't have waited ten minutes before starting Mr Lewis's operation?'

'Hamish didn't want to run overtime—you know how the theatre task force comes down hard when we run over. Besides, today is one day we both need to finish on time.' Leesa tucked her white blouse into her navy, thigh-length skirt.

'Why?'

'Family celebrations. As he said, it's our siblings' second wedding anniversary tonight and we've both been invited around for dinner.'

'A big family do.'

'Well, both sets of parents are overseas at the moment. They're all archaeologists so they're invariably out of the country. No, it will just be Angus and Janet, but Janet is a stickler for punctuality. Then, of course, there's Charlotte. She's our niece.'

'How old?'

'Ten months old today and almost walking. She's an adorable little girl with strawberry blonde hair like her mummy and blue eyes like her daddy.' Leesa undid her hair from the tight bun she always wore to Theatre before brushing it out to shoulder length, its shimmering gold glistening in the artificial lights of the changing room.

'What a lovely colour. Natural, too, I guess.' Caroline fluffed her fingers through her own short, brown hair.

'Yes.' Leesa smiled. 'Sorry to disappoint you.'

'Oh, you haven't. We middle-aged married women are used to the likes of you gorgeous single blondes.'

Leesa laughed and Caroline joined in. 'You're hardly middle-aged.'

'Pushing forty with a vengeance,' Caroline pronounced.

'Listen, I have to get to clinic but how about we catch up and have lunch next week?'

'Sounds great. Have a good time tonight.'

'Thanks.' Leesa left the theatre block and walked down the corridor to the outpatient clinic. It bothered her slightly that Caroline had a less than complimentary opinion of Hamish. Leesa, of all people, knew his shortcomings but had always made allowances for them.

She'd wanted to tell Caroline that Hamish didn't take credit for her own achievements but that he sometimes used that pompous attitude as a cover-up for his true feelings.

During the past two years, Leesa had realised that Hamish's real problem was that he refused to allow himself to feel, to get in touch with his emotions. She thought back to the years she'd known him and not once had she seen him lose his temper, get angry or upset. He was always controlled.

She supposed it had something to do with his previous marriage, but as she knew little of the particulars it was only supposition. At that point in her life, she *had* looked upon Hamish as a brother figure. She'd been far too busy with the rigmarole of high school to worry about his failing marriage.

Hamish was, to all intents and purposes, a dedicated pro-fessional—bound to serve his patients to the best of his ability.

Leesa hadn't been aiming to equal his score in her final exam—she'd wanted to beat him. Her academic achievements were the only way she received his undivided attention and, although she'd given him a wide berth over the past two years, he'd offered to help her study when finals time had arrived.

They'd swatted together for one entire weekend when he'd continuously and patiently helped her remember and learn. When he'd learned of her result, she was sure a look of shock had crossed his face. Little Leesa? As smart as himself?

Applying for the research fellowship had been solely her own idea. She'd convinced herself it had been because she had an interest in the 'long bones' of the body, even though this had just happened to be Hamish's sub-speciality. She'd convinced herself that being the research fellow of the clinical director of Orthopaedics would look very good on her résumé.

Yet all the while Leesa had known she was lying to herself. She had applied to be near Hamish again. He hadn't completely broken her heart two years previously with his unpassionate revelations—just sprained it a little. Leesa had worked harder on control over her emotions but had realised she might as well stop breathing before she would ever manage to succeed.

Caroline had been right when she'd accused him of being overbearing and arrogant—but everyone had their faults.

Hamish O'Donnell was the man for her. Her soul mate. Now all she had to do…was convince him.

CHAPTER TWO

'LEESA,' Janet called out as the doorbell rang. 'Can you get that?'

Leesa did as her sister asked and opened the door.

'Sorry I'm late,' Hamish apologised as he entered the house. 'I was caught on the phone.'

'Nothing serious, I hope,' Leesa said as they walked down the hallway and into the comfortable lounge room. After their wedding, Angus and Janet had moved from the duplex home they'd lived in and had bought a renovated five-bedroom home which wasn't too far from their consulting rooms.

'No. It was just about the American conference in June. Speaking of which, would you like to present a research paper? I think it would be a great introduction for you as my fellow. I've had four papers accepted so you could present one or two of them.'

'I'll give it some thought,' Leesa answered, trying not to commit herself to anything. The conference was an annual one on new and improved breakthroughs in orthopaedic research and was attended by everyone who was anyone. If she went, she would be spending two weeks in close proximity with Hamish and she wondered if her restraint could hold out. But that was at least four months away. Who knew what would happen in that time?

'Hey, bro,' Angus said as he entered the room. The two men shook hands.

'Where's Janet?'

'Just changing Charlotte. Here, let me get you a drink. Leesa, would you like a refill?'

'No, thanks,' Leesa answered, her wineglass still half-full.

Angus stopped suddenly on his way to the bar and groaned. Hamish and Leesa looked at each other before turning their attention back to Angus.

'Are you all right?' Hamish asked.

Angus released the breath he was holding. 'I'm fine. I think I have a bit of food poisoning. There was a lunch on at the university today—I must have eaten something that didn't agree with me.'

When he continued pouring Hamish a drink, Leesa slowly relaxed. Perhaps it *was* just food poisoning.

'If your pain continues, get it checked out.'

'Yes, big brother,' Angus said with a mischievous grin.

Leesa smiled and sat down in one of the comfortable lounges. She watched the two brothers talk shop for a while. With Angus being a doctor, but a 'simple GP', as he termed it, he was always interested in what was happening at the hospital. As well as doing a bit of research and lecturing at the university, Leesa knew Angus loved every minute of the family practice he and Janet ran together. To look at him now, no one would ever have guessed that her brother-in-law had lived a jet-setting life, changing jobs every six months to investigate fraudulent activities from research grants and clinical trials.

Then he'd come back home to Newcastle for six months and had worked with Janet. It had taken only a few months for the two of them to realise they were made for each other.

Leesa wasn't excluded from their conversation but in this instance preferred to watch the brothers as they conversed. They had many similar mannerisms, but where Hamish was always constant in his emotions Angus was like a roller-coaster. He was vehement and unbending at times and although quick to temper, it also cooled rapidly.

She could see why her sister had fallen for him. Leesa

loved Angus because he made her sister and her niece happy. As far as brothers-in-law went, he was the best. Her sole conviction for believing Hamish to be a most passionate man, although he'd hidden this side from the world, was based on Angus and his parents.

The O'Donnells were so animated and enthusiastic about life that she failed to see how Hamish wasn't. Perhaps his family's habits of overstating and overreacting had caused him to control his emotions.

The key. She sipped her wine, her eyes taking in every movement he made. Once she had the right key, she could unlock Hamish's heart. Over the years she'd tried a multitude of scenarios. She'd flaunted her dates in front of him but he'd simply wished her the best and never gave advice on her love life. She'd tried staying away, hoping absence would have made his heart yearn for hers—it hadn't worked. After his comment about her legs at her sister's wedding, she'd decided to wear skirts, hoping to attract his attention. *That* was her current plan, so she'd see how well it worked over the next few weeks.

Patience, she told herself. Patience and time—then Hamish would be hers.

'Sorry,' Janet apologised as she came into the room, carrying Charlotte. She crossed to Hamish and kissed him. 'Good to see you.'

Hamish gave Charlotte a tickle, receiving a big beaming smile from the small child in return. His eyes flashed with happiness but it was quickly veiled and Leesa shook her head in disgust. If adorable and innocent little Charlotte couldn't break through his barriers, what made her think *she* could?

Janet handed Charlotte over to her father, before asking Leesa to help her in the kitchen. While they put the finishing touches to the meal Janet had prepared, Leesa listened to her sister's new project.

'A community medicine awareness programme is just

what we need around here. Two other general practices in the district are also getting involved.'

'What does it entail?' Leesa asked with interest.

'One full day during the week and half a day on Saturdays. To start with, those doctors who are training as instructors will be attending a course run at the university on how to approach the community, and so on. Once that's completed, it's a matter of getting out there with the people—at playgroups, kindergartens, schools, community centres—and raising the awareness of basic hygiene as well as simple medical practices which can be employed in the home.'

'Sounds great. I've heard of this programme before but it will be great to hear about it from your perspective as you go through it.'

'Charlotte was my only worry.'

'The extra work?'

'No, I can cope with that. At the moment I'm working three days a week at the surgery and Charlotte is getting a bit more…shall we say…independent…' Janet smiled '…than when she was smaller. I can't keep taking her in with me. Karen, our secretary/receptionist, has had a great time looking after her, and the side room we changed into a nursery has basically served its purpose.'

'Babies have a way of growing and developing,' Leesa pointed out.

'How true that statement is.' Janet shook her head. 'I can't believe where the time has gone. It seems like just yesterday we were bringing our newborn back from the hospital. I'm going to miss having her at the surgery, but I've come up with a solution.'

'Do tell,' Leesa urged.

'I'm going to cut down to two days consulting so I can do this course. Then I'm still only working three days per week—three and a half if you count the Saturday—but

Angus will be with Charlotte during that time. You know Andrew McNeil?'

'The doctor who you were going to take on as partner before Angus decided he desperately wanted not only the job but you as well?'

Janet laughed. 'That's the one. We've all come to a mutual arrangement that he'll work permanently for us to cover whatever days I need, instead of the locum work he's been doing. He wants to cut down a few hours so it works out great. That's the consulting angle covered.'

'And Charlotte?'

'During the days I'll be away I've employed a nanny to come here and look after Charlotte in her own environment.' Janet's smile was one of extreme happiness.

'Who's the nanny?'

'Jess Masterson's daughter.'

'Gabrielle? How old is she now?'

'Just turned nineteen. Finished high school last year, is doing part-time university and has some extra time to help me out. It fell into place so neatly it was meant to be.'

'Wow. She's grown up quickly. It seems only yesterday she was just starting school.'

'I'm really comfortable with her. Apart from the fact that I know her parents, she's very natural with Charlotte and really cares about her.'

'That's great, Janet. Peace of mind means everything.'

'Do you have peace of mind in your new job?' Janet asked as they began to dish the meal out.

'Yes. It's great.'

'Speaking of great, you look lovely tonight,' her sister remarked.

'Thank you, but this *is* a special occasion.'

'That deep royal blue looks stunning on you—matches your eyes. It also shows off your legs beautifully, not to mention the rest of your body. What type of material is that?'

'Raw silk, Janet,' Leesa replied, shaking her head in amusement. 'You're a brilliant doctor, cook, housekeeper, wife and mother, to name but a few of your talents, but as far as dressmaking goes...' Leesa shook her head. 'Not *my* sister.'

'I leave the sewing up to you. I know how much it relaxes you—*when* you have the time.'

'Which will probably be even less this year.'

'Working with Hamish? Two workaholics working together. Bad news, if you ask me.'

'What's so wrong with it?' Leesa asked defensively.

'Darling, there's nothing wrong with it,' Janet said placatingly. 'Especially if you can get Hamish to come out from under his shell and realise what's in front of him.' Janet took her sister's hand in hers. 'I just don't want him to hurt you again.'

'It wouldn't matter even if he did—I'd still come back for more. I'm a masochist.' Leesa shrugged. 'Thanks for caring.'

'Hey. You're my baby sister, he's my brother-in-law. How could I not care?'

'I guess. Now, come on. Let's eat this scrumptious meal you've prepared for us.'

They all enjoyed a relaxing evening, Leesa receiving lots of cuddles and kisses from Charlotte. She doted on her niece as it was the closest she'd get, for a while, to having a child of her own. Janet let her give Charlotte her evening bottle then Leesa rocked the baby to sleep.

'Let me take her from you,' Angus offered once Charlotte was deep in dreamland, but Leesa refused.

'I like to cuddle her,' she confessed. 'It's a rare privilege.'

'You look so natural with her in your arms,' Janet remarked.

After another hour of pleasant conversation, Leesa began yawning and quickly apologised.

'My boss had me working especially hard today.' She smiled at Hamish.

'That's a bit harsh, considering it was your first day,' Angus teased, and gave his brother a hearty grin. 'Slave-driver. Don't you work my sister-in-law too hard or she'll complain to my wife who will then complain to me and I'll be forced to come and give you a talking-to.'

'I'll keep it in mind,' Hamish promised with a nod. 'As we have a busy day planned for tomorrow, I suggest Leesa and I leave you to celebrate your wedding anniversary in true honeymoon fashion.'

'Thank you, Hamish. How very thoughtful.' Janet grinned and hugged her husband close.

'Let me put Charlotte in her cot.' Leesa stood and carried the sleeping child to her room and, after kissing her good-night, laid the baby down to rest. Watching her for a moment, Leesa heard a strange ticking sound in her mind and realised it was her biological clock. Time, she told herself again. She just needed a bit more time.

Hamish and Leesa said their goodbyes to Janet and Angus, thanking them for a lovely evening, before walking to Leesa's car.

'You look lovely, as usual,' Hamish told her, his eyes never leaving her face. 'Did you make the dress?' They stopped beside her car and looked at each other, the star-lit night evoking a romantic mood.

'Yes.' Leesa held her breath, searching for hidden meaning in his words.

'I thought so. It fits you like a glove.'

Leesa was beginning to look beyond the blandness of his tone. Teasing him seemed like her best option at the moment. That and a little bit of physical contact.

'Flattery, Hamish, will get you everywhere.' She reached out and quickly took his hand before he realised what she was up to. 'See...' she pointed out as she held his hand firmly against her waist and then slid it down to rest at the top of her thigh. 'You were right. It does fit like a glove.'

To her astonishment and delight, Leesa saw his Adam's apple work overtime as he swallowed convulsively. A flash of longing pierced his cool blue eyes then disappeared, but Leesa had seen it.

'As I knew it would,' he replied with control, although he made no attempt to remove his hand. To have done so would have been an indication that he was affected by her actions. He waited another heart-stopping moment, his warm hand seeming to burn into her flesh, his thumb moving, oh, so slightly in a small circle.

Almost reluctantly, he said, 'I need my hand back in order to drive home.'

Feeling triumphant, Leesa allowed him the concession.

'Goodnight, Leesa.' He nodded briefly. 'I'll see you early tomorrow morning at the hospital.'

She watched him cross the road to his waiting Jaguar Sovereign, then waved cheerfully as he drove down the street.

Still smiling, Leesa drove to her apartment near the hospital. Hamish had acknowledged her! That brief look in his eyes had been similar to the one she'd witnessed exactly two years ago at the wedding.

It was what she'd been waiting for again. A sign. An indication that he still desired her. And tonight, through putting her own reservations aside, she'd discovered his feelings were still there.

Whether he spoke with a calm and clear voice was now of no concern to her. His emotions were there, simmering beneath the surface, as she'd always surmised.

'Get ready, Hamish O'Donnell,' she warned him as she brushed her hair before bed. 'Cold showers will be the only remedy for your aching body once I'm finished with you.'

* * *

On Saturday night—or more correctly Sunday morning—
two weeks after her sister's dinner, Leesa and Hamish sat
in the emergency theatre doctors' lounge, waiting impatiently for the ambulance to arrive with another load of
casualties. A huge motorcycle pile-up on the Newcastle
Expressway had resulted in multiple casualties. The Sydney
hospitals were so full that a number of patients were being
airlifted to Newcastle General.

'Would you like another cup?' Leesa asked as she took
their empty coffee-cups to the sink.

'If I have another one, I'll start to drown,' Hamish remarked with a lopsided grin. He stood and started to pace
slowly around the room. 'Thanks, anyway.'

'The waiting is the hardest part.' Leesa yawned and
stretched her hands up over her head. They'd already been
in Theatre for the past six hours, and as it was now almost
three o'clock in the morning she knew neither of them
would get any real sleep until much later.

Lowering her arms, she turned to ask Hamish a question
but found him staring at her body. He quickly lifted his
gaze to her face and what she saw there erased any previous
fatigue she might have been feeling.

His blue eyes were molten pools of desire, his lips were
slightly parted and one hand was being raked nervously
through his hair.

'Perhaps waiting in here…' he indicated the small room
which was set up with comfortable chairs, a few side tables
and tea and coffee facilities '…wasn't such a good idea
after all,' he muttered, before breaking eye contact.

Leesa was too tired to play his games any longer.
'Hamish.' She sat down in a chair and looked at him. He
had his back to her and was looking intently at a picture
on the wall.

'Hamish,' she repeated, and he turned around. 'Why…
why do you keep fighting the attraction you feel for me?'

He was silent for such a long time that she thought he might not answer her. Finally he shrugged and said, 'It's just not natural, Leesa. I've watched you grow up, guided you, advised you. You're like a sister to me.'

What a breakthrough, she thought, but schooled her facial expression. At least he acknowledged *something* between them. That was a start. Leesa knew if she pushed and poked too hard, she'd drive him away for good. Taking a deep breath, she said firmly,

'I am *not* your sister, Hamish, and the sooner you get that through your thick skull, the sooner we can move on with our lives.' She stood and walked slowly towards him. 'You say it isn't natural—your feelings for me. Why? What's so wrong with them?'

'Leesa, please, let's not discuss this. Not now. We have several ambulances full of patients coming our way and you want to talk about *sex.*'

'Sex?' Leesa stopped walking and smiled slowly at him. 'Why, Hamish,' she teased, 'I hadn't even thought about that—but you obviously have.'

'Leesa,' he implored again.

The door to the doctors' lounge opened and Caroline Metcalfe came in. 'They're due to arrive at any moment, so if you would like to take your places the games can begin.'

'Thank you, Sister Metcalfe,' Hamish replied, and quickly walked past Leesa, out to Casualty.

'You OK?' Caroline asked Leesa.

'I'm better than OK.' Leesa smiled, ecstatic with Hamish's small admissions. 'Come on, let's get this night over and done with.'

The wail of the ambulance sirens could be heard approaching and the triage team and all available staff were at the ready. Theatres were scrubbed and waiting for the patients who would all, hopefully, make it through the next few hours.

Hamish went from one patient to the next, ordering X-rays and prescribing drugs. Leesa followed him, making sure the red tape was taken care of by signing the necessary request forms and casenotes. If they didn't do it immediately, to ensure everything was above board, something might be missed. Procedures and protocols were in place for a reason. If a patient filed a claim against the hospital, the paperwork needed to be accurately recorded and meticulously checked.

'Over here, Mr O'Donnell,' one of the triage nurses called when Hamish and Leesa had finished with their latest patient.

Hamish crossed the room, not a hint of fatigue about him. 'Status?'

'Unconscious Caucasian male. Stable. Multiple trauma. Compound comminuted fractures to the right femur, fractured right scapula and humerus and the pelvis is fractured in several places. Minor concussion, bruises and lacerations,' the sister reported.

'Haemodynamically stable?' Leesa asked as she continued writing up the notes and preparing X-ray forms.

'Yes,' Sister replied. 'He received three units of blood in transit.'

'X-rays of all fractures, including his head,' Hamish ordered. 'A general X-ray of the pelvis is all I need for the moment. Three-dimensional scanning can be performed at a later date.' Hamish turned and spoke quietly to Leesa. 'That femur looks dreadful. Make sure we have an all round view of the entire right leg. I don't want anything left to chance.'

'Yes, Hamish.' She quickly wrote up the forms as Hamish continued to review the patient. Leesa turned to the triage sister. 'Do we have a name for this patient? Most of the others have tattoos somewhere so we're identifying them by those markings.'

'The paramedics have written his name down as Jonno,' she informed them.

'Jonno,' Leesa repeated, and noted it down on the X-ray forms. He had long, dark hair and quite a few tattoos from what she could see. 'Analgesics?'

'Morphine was administered at the crash site after he was stabilised but that was close to four hours ago now,' sister reported.

'It should be wearing off soon. The lacerations all look fine and won't need suturing,' Hamish advised, and Leesa made notes. 'I want him in Theatre, a.s.a.p., so put a rush on all X-rays. We'll do his femur first and then take a closer look at the humerus and scapula.'

'And the pelvis?' Leesa asked.

'If the X-rays indicate the need for surgical intervention then I'll do it next week. I'll head to Theatre to organise the equipment. Once the X-rays are done, have him prepped immediately.'

'Yes, Hamish.'

He gave her a nod before walking off to Theatre, leaving her to finalise things. She called to the triage sister who had attended the patient. 'I need a radiographer immediately to X-ray Jonno. Mr O'Donnell wants him in Theatre, stat.'

'Right away, Doctor,' the sister replied as Leesa thrust the authorised notes at her.

Once the X-rays were done, Leesa found Hamish and together they reviewed them.

Hamish shook his head in amazement at the way the femur was fractured. 'It's going to be a tough one but...' he looked across at Leesa. '...we can save it.'

Leesa gave the X-rays to the scout nurse before they began scrubbing. When they entered the theatre, Jonno was being anaesthetised.

'I don't envy your job,' Pete, the anaesthetist, told Hamish.

'You don't envy *mine?* No. I don't envy yours. You have no idea what this man has been drinking or smoking. He's unconscious to begin with and you have to make sure he stays that way. No, Pete, I definitely have the easier job.'

'The man has multiple trauma, Hamish, and from what I can see of the X-rays that femur is a complete mess,' Pete pointed out. 'I don't know, Hamish. I doubt even *you* could perform a miracle on this guy. Are you really *that* good?'

Leesa could tell Pete was smiling beneath his mask, his eyes twinkling with humour. He and Hamish were old friends and it showed in their easy banter.

'Have you been reading orthopaedic textbooks again, Pete?' Leesa joked.

Pete turned his attention to her and winked. 'You noticed! I must say, Dr Stevenson, that you look ravishing today,' he told her.

'Just concentrate on your job,' Hamish growled. 'You're a married man, Pete. Don't forget it.'

Leesa tried to ignore Hamish's comments, although she was delighted with his prompt reaction to Pete's teasing.

'Thank you, Pete.' She assisted Hamish in draping the patient. 'I believe the baggy green cloth of the theatre outfit really does something for a girl. Perhaps I should contact *Vogue* and sell them my secrets.'

'Don't forget the hats,' Caroline added as she did her instrument count.

'And the masks.' Leesa laughed and Caroline joined in.

'Have you two quite finished?' Hamish growled.

'Don't get grumpy just because *you* failed to notice how attractive I am,' Leesa said. 'A woman likes to receive compliments now and then. You'd do well to remember that, Hamish.'

'Leesa!' His calm tone held a hint of warning but she could read in his eyes that her teasing had hit a sore spot. Good, she thought, and about time, too.

'The patient is ready when you are, Hamish,' Pete announced.

'Thank you,' Hamish replied, a hint of fatigue in his tone. The strain of the past twelve hours was beginning to take its toll on all of them, but they had a few more hours to get through before they were finished. Everyone in the hospital was doing his or her job to the best of their ability and no one could ask for more. Even Hamish.

'Right,' he said clearly for the entire theatre staff to hear. 'We'll be stabilising the femur with a Grosse and Kempf intramedullary nail, which will be placed down through the centre of the bone, thereby stabilising it. The other fragments will be screwed back into place, using a combination of plates, screws and wires. If you have any questions, ask. We're all tired and exhausted but that's no excuse for incompetence.'

He waited for a brief moment, before saying, 'Let's get to work.'

After he'd finished with the G and K nail, he said, 'I need a check X-ray on the femur before I can continue.'

Caroline nodded to the scout nurse. 'Radiographer and portable X-ray machine in here, stat.'

'Yes, Sister,' the scout nurse replied, and got busy organising things.

'We don't have a machine in here ready to go?' Hamish asked. His tone was quiet but held a hint of warning.

'No, Mr O'Donnell,' Caroline informed him.

'That's just…great,' he ground out between clenched teeth.

'With the state of emergencies in the hospital, Mr O'Donnell—' Caroline started to explain, but he merely held up a gloved hand for silence.

'How long?' Leesa asked, and they all turned to the scout nurse who was replacing the phone receiver.

'At least twenty minutes,' she said bravely.

Leesa heard Hamish grind his teeth even harder and she

winced inwardly. The phone shrilled to life and the scout nurse snatched it up again, a look of relief washing over her face at the timely interruption.

'I'll ask him,' she said into the receiver.

'Mr O'Donnell, your service registrar, Dr Hannover, wants to know if you're available for the patient in theatre two.'

'Speak to her, Leesa,' he said quietly, his voice still radiating impatience. Leesa walked over to the phone. The scout nurse held the receiver to her ear and Leesa listened to a nervous Dr Hannover. When she was finished she returned to Hamish's side.

'The patient has a fracture to the lower third of the right humerus, fracture dislocation of the right acetabulum and an undisplaced fracture of the left acetabulum—'

'Seems to be a night for pelvic fractures,' Hamish interrupted.

'Yes. He also has a closed head injury.'

'Have Neurology seen the patient?'

'Yes. They've given the all-clear. Dr Hannover said they were almost ready to anaesthetise the patient. They just needed to know who was free before they began.'

'Fine. Pete?' He turned his attention to the anaesthetist. 'Are you happy with Jonno's status?'

'He's doing fine.'

'Good. Leesa, you stay here and monitor Jonno. The instant the check X-ray is ready, have me paged and send it through to theatre two.'

With that, he de-gowned. Leesa followed suit and stopped him on his way out of Theatre.

'Radiology can't help it if all their machines are busy, Hamish,' she rationalised.

'I know.' He rubbed a weary hand across his forehead. 'Dr Hannover—how long has she been in the department?'

'She started the same day as me.' Leesa smiled. 'This is Roxanne Hannover's first orthopaedic service rotation. In the past two weeks she's shown competence but lack of experience, which is to be expected. She has a lot to learn but seems committed to do so. Promise me you'll go easy on her? This will be her first time alone with you since she started her rotation and she's liable to be a bit nervous.'

'So she should be. To be working alongside the great Mr O'Donnell, it should make anyone nervous. Even you.'

'Ha. That'll be the day.' Leesa laughed and Hamish smiled. 'Your ego is getting far too big, Hamish,' she told him.

Leesa loved sharing these small intimate moments with him. When it was just the two of them, there was no need for any careful behaviour. She knew Hamish didn't want anyone to think he'd shown preference in appointing her as his research fellow just because they'd known each other for so long. It made him more guarded around their colleagues.

But now, even though they were in the midst of all these emergencies, Leesa was happy to see Hamish relax for a short spell when he needed it most.

'Page me,' he ordered, before walking off.

Once the X-ray had been processed, Leesa took a good look at it while the scout nurse paged Hamish. The long nail was shown to be clearly in place. Hamish would be pleased.

She heard a faint beeping noise coming from the scrub room and looked through the window. Hamish was standing at the scrub sink. He raised his eyebrows when their eyes met but no smile was forthcoming on his lips. What was he doing here? He should still be tied up in theatre two.

'Mr O'Donnell is here and scrubbing,' she announced to the theatre, and everyone sprang into action.

'What happened?' Leesa asked quietly as Hamish studied the X-rays of the G and K nail he'd inserted into Jonno's femur. Hamish's eyes darkened slightly.

'The patient died fifteen minutes ago. Myocardial infarction just as he was being anaesthetised.'

Leesa nodded. She wondered how Dr Hannover was feeling, but for the moment she needed to push all irrelevant thoughts to the back of her mind and concentrate on the procedure at hand.

'Those X-rays look good. Let's continue,' Hamish announced to the theatre, and took his place at the table.

Once he was happy with the femur, they started work on the arm. Thankfully, the break to the scapula was relatively clean and required only a small plate and a few screws to hold it in place. The humerus required an intramedullary rush pin to ensure it was secure.

At last they were finished and apart from Jonno's pelvic fracture, which would be looked into after they'd all had some sleep, the patient was wheeled to Recovery.

Leesa and Hamish de-gowned yet again, before returning to the doctors' lounge. Leesa made them each a cup of coffee before sinking into a chair, glad to have the weight off her feet.

'What happened in theatre two?' she asked, but the instant the words were out of her mouth her beeper sounded. Dredging up the energy to answer it, she looked at the number.

'Theatre four,' she announced as she took a few gulps of her coffee. She rang through to see what was next on the list.

When she was finished she looked at Hamish. 'Theatre four has a patient with two broken arms. Open reduction and internal fixation required.'

Hamish drained his coffee-cup and stood. 'Let's go.' Leesa took a final sip of her coffee and threw the rest down the sink before they reported to theatre four.

Caroline Metcalfe had just finished scrubbing. 'We meet again.' She smiled at them both. 'See you inside.'

'Caroline Metcalfe is a very competent theatre sister,' he

remarked as they scrubbed. 'I've been working with her for over a year and I'm still highly impressed by her constant professionalism.'

'Why don't you try telling *her* that some time? A little praise can go a long way.'

'Know her that well, do you?'

'We've had lunch a few times.'

'Or are you trying to give me an indirect message?' He raised an eyebrow at her over the sink they shared.

'Let's just say the few times you've actually, albeit reluctantly, told me I've done a good job have been like flecks of gold in a river. They're exciting to find but very rare.'

Hamish elbowed the taps off and looked at her for a long moment. 'You must know I'm extremely proud of your accomplishments.'

'Yes, I do, Hamish.' Leesa turned her taps off and met his gaze. 'I feel it, I sense it, but hearing you say it does wonders for me. Your opinion matters all too much, I'm afraid.'

Hamish was silent then nodded. 'Noted for future reference.' The scrub nurse came to help them gown so further conversation was cut short.

The patient there was a large, bearded man whose arms had taken the brunt of his fall. They got to work and fixed the fractures back into place. Open reduction and internal fixation required them to fit the pieces of bone back together, securing them with plates and screws. Once the bones had knitted back together, which usually took around twelve to eighteen months, the metal would be removed.

Finally, once again, they were ready to finish and de-gown. Leesa rang through to Casualty to get an update.

'Apart from the night's events generating a mound of paperwork, the situation is stable,' Triage Sister informed her.

Dr Hannover and the two orthopaedic registrars who

were on call had taken care of the other patients. Casualty reported that most had been minor fractures, requiring either plaster casts or minor plating to fix the bones back together.

Leesa replaced the phone and turned to Hamish. 'How about some breakfast?'

'Sounds good.'

She hesitated for a split second, before saying, 'Would you like to come back to my place? It's closer than yours.'

Hamish swallowed and cleared his throat. 'Why don't we see what the hospital cafeteria is offering?'

'Sure,' Leesa replied a little too quickly. Previously, Hamish probably wouldn't have thought twice about having breakfast at her place, especially after the gruelling night they'd just shared. Those moments they'd shared in the doctors' tea-lounge had changed things.

Hamish was aware of her attraction to him, more so than he'd been in the past. Leesa now knew he wasn't as indifferent to her as he'd once been. An innocent breakfast, regardless of her motives, would now be construed as a dangerous situation as far as Hamish was concerned.

Breakfast at the hospital cafeteria. Well, she reasoned as they walked silently out of Theatres, at least she'd be sharing it with Hamish.

CHAPTER THREE

'MAY I sit here?' a voice asked from behind her.

'Sure, why not?' Leesa asked rhetorically. Where had she formed the idea that breakfast in the hospital cafeteria with Hamish would be better than nothing? She wasn't having breakfast with Hamish! He was heavy in discussion with one of his registrars about the night's events. Indeed, the entire *table,* consisting of thirty chairs, was involved in a discussion about the work they'd all been doing throughout the night.

The cafeteria, which was usually more subdued at this time of morning, was swarming with hungry staff and there were now very few places left to sit.

Dr Hannover sat down next to Leesa, who had finished her breakfast of pancakes and fruit, and handed her a fresh cup of coffee.

'Here. You looked as though you could use this.'

'Thanks.' Leesa turned to face the other woman and accepted the cup. She noticed that Roxanne's hand wasn't quite steady, although none of the hot liquid spilled.

'Are you all right, Roxanne?'

The young doctor looked surprised. 'I didn't realise you knew my first name,' she said as she sipped her own coffee.

'You're the only other female on the orthopaedic staff. We have to stick together.' Leesa smiled, hoping to put Roxanne at ease.

'How did you decide that orthopaedics was for you?' Roxanne asked quietly, not wanting too many people to hear their conversation.

Leesa thought for a moment. 'I guess Hamish made it

sound so vibrant, so compelling that it was a natural progression for me to follow.'

'Hamish?' Roxanne asked, clearly puzzled.

'Mr O'Donnell,' Leesa replied softly, her smile increasing. 'Our families have been friends for years,' she added, by way of explaining the familiar relationship she had with the head of department. 'He has been my mentor throughout my career, now he's my boss. Ironic, if you ask me, but that's the way it is.'

'Was he…? Is he…mad…at…?' Roxanne stopped, took another sip of her coffee and tried again. 'That man…the patient…who…the one who died…' She broke off again and raised her cup back to her lips.

Leesa waited.

'It wasn't my fault.' Her words were barely audible in the clattering and banging of the cafeteria, but Leesa heard them.

Leesa glanced across at Hamish who appeared to be engrossed in listening to his registrar, but then his gaze flicked ever so briefly to meet hers before he inclined his head towards the door.

There was no way he could have heard their conversation but, by observing Dr Hannover's behaviour, he'd known there was something wrong.

'Why don't we go to my office?' Leesa suggested quietly.

The two women stood and Leesa collected their coffee-cups. 'Excuse me,' she interrupted Hamish. 'I'll see you soon.'

'Yes, you will.' Hamish nodded and gave his attention back to his registrar.

The sudden silence of the corridor hit them like a brick. 'Whew! It sure is noisy in there,' Leesa remarked, trying to make idle conversation. She guessed that Dr Hannover was probably close to tears but wanted to delay them until they were in the privacy of Leesa's office.

When they arrived, Leesa placed their coffee-cups on the table, then offered Roxanne a chair. Leesa perched on the edge of her desk and waited. When Roxanne didn't say anything, Leesa said softly, 'I have no idea what happened in Theatre, Roxanne.'

'Mr O'Donnell didn't tell you?' She lifted her head and looked at Leesa in surprise.

'No time to discuss it. It's been a pretty hectic stint in Theatre for all of us.' Leesa waited a few more seconds then urged gently, 'Why don't you tell me what happened?'

'He...' She stopped, her voice choking on a sob. 'He...' She tried again but the floodgates opened and Roxanne began to cry. Leesa quickly reached for some tissues and handed them to her, before kneeling beside the distraught woman and gently placing a hand on her shoulder. 'Shh,' she consoled, but knew the best thing for Roxanne was to cry it out of her system.

'I've seen death before...but not a heart attack. Not like that.' Roxanne sniffed a while later and dried her eyes. Leesa stood and resumed her position, leaning against the table. While Roxanne blew her nose Leesa reached for the telephone, tapped in a number, then replaced the receiver.

'The cadaver in medical school didn't make me faint or vomit or anything,' the service registrar clarified. 'It was just my scientific teacher. I've seen a patient being removed from life support, all sorts of things—but not in Theatre. In Recovery, yes, but not in Theatre. I didn't even *know* the man and here I am, crying as though he was my closest friend in the world. It's ridiculous.'

'Death has a way of making us stop and think. What if it had been me? What if it had been someone I'm close to?' Leesa responded.

'I just feel as though I could have done something more,' Roxanne stressed. 'Why didn't I do an ECG before he was admitted to Theatre? Perhaps that would have shown he had a weak heart. Or…' She stopped, tears welling in her eyes again.

'Take a deep breath and start from the beginning,' Leesa instructed.

'Everything was going along fine. Mr O'Donnell and I had just finished looking at the X-rays and were starting to scrub.' She shook her head. 'It all seemed to happen so quickly. We heard the sister who was assisting the anaesthetist call that the patient's blood pressure was rising rapidly just as the anaesthetist was about to intubate. The patient started having a seizure and Mr O'Donnell and I came rushing in.

'By this stage, the patient had stopped breathing and Mr O'Donnell started cardiac massage. The anaesthetist pumped oxygen in through the mouth while the theatre sister grabbed the crash cart. That's when things really hit me and I managed to snap my attention back to reality and join my colleagues.'

She paused and looked at Leesa. 'It's the first time I've had to apply the defibrillator paddles. Mr O'Donnell called for them again and again and each time there was no result. I kept willing the man to live. Each time I applied those paddles I wanted his heart to start up again and then everything would be all right.'

'Did the patient appear to be in a high-risk category for heart attack?' Leesa asked when Roxanne had been silent for a few minutes.

'Yes,' the other woman nodded sadly. 'He was very overweight, teeth were stained from nicotine and it was written in his notes that his pupils were dilated at the accident site, indicating substance abuse.'

'Did the notes say that he'd regained consciousness at any time since the accident?'

'No.'

'From the list of fractures he had, there could have been all sorts of complications involved, which was why Theatre was necessary. Neurology had passed him as being safe to anaesthetise so, from what you've said, there's no way anyone could have pre-empted this situation. As far as the hospital is concerned, all protocols have been followed, but the autopsy will confirm the actual cause of death. There's no point in trying to second-guess yourself,' Leesa pointed out as she stood. 'Not in this instance.'

'Does this mean that I'm not cut out for a career in surgery?' Roxanne asked.

'Only you can be the judge of that. How did you cope with your internship rotation?'

'Fine. I quite enjoyed my time in orthopaedics and with other specialities that required a lot of theatre work.'

'Is that why you decided to do a year as an orthopaedic service registrar?'

'Yes. But after last night…'

'If *you* would like a transfer, I can arrange it, but I think you'd be better off staying here for the year,' Leesa suggested. 'Tonight was frantic, to say the least, and it *will* happen again.' She took a deep breath, hoping what she wanted to say would come out in the right vein. 'Being a good doctor—or surgeon, for that matter—requires more than skill, as I'm sure you've come to realise. I'm sure Mr O'Donnell is also upset about the patient but it sounds as though the staff did everything they could. It was no one's fault. No one is to blame. When he went into cardiac arrest, *everything* was done to bring him back to life, but sometimes it just doesn't work.

'When things like this happen, all we can do is push it to the back of our minds and get on with saving other lives, operating on those patients who still need our expertise.'

'I feel so…numb.'

'It's to be expected. You may even feel this way for the next few days. As doctors, it's natural that we care, that the loss of any patient affects us in some way and that we find a way to deal with it—to go on and continue in this vocation we've been called to.'

There was a brief knock at her door before it opened and Hamish walked in. Roxanne seemed embarrassed by his presence and straightened her back, hiding the tell-tale tissues.

'Everything OK?' he asked with concern, pulling a chair around to sit opposite Roxanne.

'I didn't want Dr Stevenson to bother you, sir.'

'It's her job to bother me,' Hamish quipped, but smiled to belie the severity of his words. Leesa watched as he worked his magic over the young doctor, his charm relaxing her.

'Besides, when a member of my staff is in need of attention, then I like to know they receive it.' He paused for a moment. 'It wasn't your fault.' He had known, without being told, exactly what the problem was. 'You did everything correctly. Your job as service registrar is to assist and learn. We were short-staffed and inundated with casualties last night. In essence, you were thrown in at the deep end and still handled it well.'

Roxanne sighed and allowed a small smile to light her face. 'Thank you. It means a lot to hear you say that.' She stood. 'Thank you, too, Dr Stevenson,' she added.

'My pleasure.'

'I'd better get going.' Roxanne opened the door, then turned back. 'I...I don't want a transfer. I think I'll stick around and see what orthopaedics has to teach me.'

'Wise decision,' Leesa answered, before the young doctor left the room.

'What took you so long?' Hamish asked quietly the instant the door was closed.

'What do you mean?'

'Damian Wright had me cornered, discussing all the patients he'd operated on in the past twelve hours in painstaking detail. I thought you were going to page me the second you left the cafeteria but, no, I had to endure another five minutes—at least—of hearing him tell me how brilliant he is.'

Leesa laughed. 'He's a good doctor but I know what you mean. Sorry. Roxanne was a bit teary and you would have embarrassed her even more.'

'That's a sexist comment to make.'

'But it's true.'

'Can't you show even a little bit of remorse?' He held his thumb and forefinger an inch apart.

Leesa laughed, loving this teasing side of Hamish. 'So you'd prefer me to lie to you?'

'I didn't say that—but perhaps you could, you know, once in a while, just stretch the truth a little? Make *me* feel as though I'm needed amongst my staff, instead of waltzing in here and taking over. You've only been here two weeks, Leesa, and already you're running the department.'

'Oh.' Leesa feigned surprise. 'Isn't that what I was supposed to do? After all, I am your right-hand...er...man.' She raised her eyebrows suggestively.

At her words, Hamish swallowed, his gaze roaming slowly over her body. He cleared his throat. 'You are...no *man,* Leesa. Believe me.'

The atmosphere around them changed from one of shared camaraderie to being thick with tension.

Leesa briefly closed her eyes, attempting to control the rapid increase of her pulse. She knew something important was about to happen and her tongue involuntarily ran itself over her bottom lip in anticipation.

She heard Hamish groan and opened her eyes. They stared at each other for a long minute before Leesa straightened up from the desk and took a step towards the chair in which he sat.

He seemed mesmerised by her as she came to stand before him, her breasts level with his face. As though in slow motion, Hamish reached out a hand and placed it hesitantly

on the back of her thigh, before allowing it to move upwards to cup her bottom.

All the air in Leesa's lungs whooshed out. The tumult
of emotions his caress evoked was incredible. This was the
first time Hamish had *ever* touched her in such a way and
she knew it was a dramatic step forward in their burgeoning
relationship.

Leesa wasn't sure what to do next so she stood perfectly
still and waited, the excitement spiralling throughout her
body, growing with each passing second. She looked down
into his eyes which were glazed with pent-up passion and
desire.

The sudden urge to simply haul him out of the chair and
onto her desk, before making wild, uncontrollable love to
him, was something she had to fight. She *had* to allow him
to progress at his pace. Trying to rush Hamish, she had
learned over the years, would only result in him retreating,
slamming on the brakes, and that was the *last* thing Leesa
wanted.

Fighting for stronger control, Leesa revelled in his touch
as his other hand came to rest at her waist. This hand
moved upwards over her ribcage and when his thumb, ever
so slightly, brushed the edge of her breast Leesa's eyes
fluttered closed and she sighed with longing, needing, wanting.

'Leesa...' he whispered, his tone holding a note of un-
certainty.

'Shh.' She placed a finger against his lips to silence him.
Hamish gently nipped at her finger, drawing it between his
lips. His tongue leisurely circled it, before sucking it deeper
into his mouth.

Leesa's breathing was hard and furious from his seductive assault on her finger. She felt his hand at her back urge
her forward. Her legs were already pressing hard against
the chair—how much closer did he want her?

As she leaned against him, Hamish wrapped his arms

around her back and buried his head in her breasts. Leesa reached out to thrust her hands into his hair, holding him firmly in place. In all her wildest fantasies about this man she had always known the *real* Hamish would be a million times better than anything she could dream up.

'Oh, Hamish. Hamish.' She whispered his name in wonderment, overwhelmed with her body's response.

Her words caused him to pull back and look up at her. Leesa watched as the glazed desire in his eyes slowly disappeared, and dropped her hands back to her sides. He let her go as though she'd burnt him and stood up so quickly that the chair crashed to the floor.

'Leesa. I don't know—'

'Don't you dare apologise,' Leesa warned, her voice amazingly calm as she tried to repress the passion he'd so abruptly broken.

'But, Leesa…you're—'

'I'm what, Hamish?' Her tone was firm as she realised she had to get her point across once and for all. 'Am I your long-time family friend? Your surrogate little sister? The girl you've mentored for most of her life? No. Not any more. I'm Leesa. A person in my own right. I'm a woman, Hamish, and, although you find it difficult to admit, you are irrepressibly attracted to me. We belong together…we make sense.

'You weren't holding the girl you tutored through high school, or the medical student you mentored. You weren't holding the registrar you pushed to exceed her own goals, neither were you holding the qualified orthopaedic surgeon who is now your research fellow. You were holding *me*. Wanting *me*. Desiring *me*. Me—the woman whose body aches for you. The woman who knows how perfect we are for one another. The woman who is standing before you.'

'Leesa. It's wron—'

'Don't say it's wrong, Hamish. It isn't. It's right. It's never been so right between two people as it is between you and me. We fit. We connect. Not just physically but emotionally, mentally and spiritually. We are each other's half.'

Hamish ran a hand through his hair and then crossed his arms in front of his chest—defensively—as though he couldn't trust himself not to haul her against him once more.

'You can keep on denying it if you like but you're only kidding yourself. You need me, as much as you need the air to breathe. I'll give you time and I'll give you space but I won't be patient for ever. Nor will I hide my attraction for you any longer.'

'You're fatigued.'

'Don't make excuses for me. I may be tired but I'm in complete control of my faculties.'

She looked at him. They were both still in green theatre scrubs. His hair was dishevelled, his face was drawn and tired and his whole body was rigid from the uncontrollable emotions he was unsuccessfully fighting. He had never looked more handsome in all the time she'd known him.

'I think we both need to get changed and get some sleep,' he said finally, forcing control of the situation back into his own corner. 'Thankfully it's Sunday and we don't have any clinics to contend with. After a quick ward round, I suggest it's time for bed.'

'Alone?' she couldn't resist asking, her tone teasing. Hamish glared at her and she held her hands up in defence.

'Alone,' he reiterated firmly.

'Whatever you say, Hamish,' she replied meekly before opening her office door and walking out, leaving him to follow. Even though she wouldn't be there in body, Leesa knew that after what had just transpired Hamish wouldn't be able to get her out of his mind. The knowledge left her feeling triumphant.

Hamish wearily unlocked the door to his apartment and went inside. He made it to the sofa, before collapsing thankfully onto the cushioned comfort. What a night! What a morning! What a woman!

Leesa was becoming far too close for her own good. How was he going to get it through her thick skull that it just wouldn't work between them? He was attracted to her—he had been for years—but there was more to a relationship than that.

He reflected on how incredible she'd felt in his arms. How soft and compliant she'd been. He'd always known the *real* Leesa would be everything and more than his dreams about her.

Hamish knew he must put a stop to her games. They should both learn from his drastic mistake—his first marriage.

Leesa had been in high school at the time and of no interest to Hamish, not in the physical sense. She'd been a bright kid and he'd wanted to make sure she succeeded. Back then had been the time he *had* viewed Leesa as a surrogate sister.

She knew little of his marriage to Sandra. In fact, he wasn't even sure if she'd met his ex-wife. Sandra, too, had been a close friend of his. They'd met at medical school and had become study partners. It had slowly progressed into more and at the end of their internship, Sandra had impulsively suggested they get married. Hamish had been swept up in her enthusiasm and had agreed.

He'd been young, he rationalised, but for years had always regretted the decision. The marriage had lasted under six months as Sandra had begun to realise that 'playing house' had been more than she'd been able to cope with.

He'd come home from a night similar to the one they'd just had. Emergencies everywhere. Sandra had been due to return from a conference in Melbourne and he'd expected to find her at their apartment, asleep in their bed.

Instead, there had been a message on the answering machine, informing him that she wasn't coming back and would contact her solicitor about a divorce.

At first he'd been furious but after a few days he'd come to realise it was the best possible outcome for both of them. In hindsight, Hamish knew he'd had a lucky escape, even though he'd been committed to try and work at his marriage.

Sandra was the complete opposite of Leesa—even in physical appearance. Sandra had been dark and exotic, whereas Leesa was like a ray of sunshine. Sandra and he had disagreed on many a topic, whereas Leesa appeared to be of a similar mind and nature to himself. Certainly Leesa was his intellectual equal and he'd never doubted her potential.

His ex-wife, as far as he knew, was still a general practitioner. When he'd suggested she do further study to improve her skills—offer a wider variety of treatments to her patients—she'd refused. Although he'd found nothing wrong with that, Sandra had been unable to fathom why he'd chosen to pursue orthopaedics.

Instead of agreeing to disagree, Sandra had hounded him at every possible moment on the topic until it had obviously become too much for her. Why couldn't he be content to just be a general practitioner rather than a surgeon? Why couldn't they earn some 'real' money rather than endure another five or six years of orthopaedic training?

Their friendship had been ruined and the last he'd heard she'd set up a medical practice in an exclusive suburb of Melbourne and was happy.

It was all he'd needed to hear and any previous guilt or responsibility he'd felt for her had ended. He was now a complete stranger to the woman he'd married, the woman he'd once had such a strong friendship with.

'Learn from your mistakes,' Hamish said out loud into the stillness of the room. His friendship with Leesa was too precious to jeopardise.

He sat on the sofa for a few more minutes before realising that if he didn't move soon he'd inevitably fall asleep and wake with a sore neck or back, or both. Standing, he walked into his bedroom, stripping off his clothes as he went.

Glad he'd showered at the hospital, he pulled back the sheets of the neatly made bed and climbed in. Resting his head on the pillows, he closed his eyes but his mind was too active for sleep.

He breathed in deeply, recalling all too easily the scent of Leesa's perfume. The softness of her body, the feel of her in his arms. Her hair, her eyes, her smile. Everything about the woman drove him to distraction. The worst thing was, he knew Leesa felt that same distraction.

It was up to him to be the responsible one. He must work through this. Control his urges. He had in the past so why should this be any different?

Because Leesa was pushing. The instant he'd allowed her to see the spark of desire he'd managed to hide for so long, she'd set her target lock onto him like an expert marksman.

Now she wouldn't *stop* pushing—she'd even told him as much. Hamish didn't know how much longer he could hold out against her persuasive charms. She'd said she'd give him time—but that she wouldn't wait for ever.

What would happen if he allowed nature to take its course and stopped running? Would the relationship fizzle out after a few short weeks? Months? Once their curiosity had been satisfied—what then?

'No.' He punched his pillow as he said the word. Leesa was too important to him. Important as the small girl he'd watched grow into a stunning, sensual woman. Important as the friend and colleague who was so dear to him. Important as his intellectual equal.

She was definitely marriage material and Hamish knew she wouldn't settle for anything less. Yet considering he'd vowed *never* to marry again, he'd end up hurting her—and there lay his dilemma.

He would *never* forgive himself if he hurt her—and that was why they could never be more than they already were.

The following day, Leesa arrived fifteen minutes late to Theatre. She'd had a terrible time getting her car started and had ended up calling a professional motor service to come and fix it. The battery was dead and she'd require a new one, the mechanic told her. Leaving it in their capable hands, she'd rung for a taxi but that had taken another ten minutes to show up. Then there had been a traffic jam on the main street between her apartment and the hospital. And she *had* planned to be at the hospital at least one hour before Theatre began. So much for plans. Perhaps she should have stayed in bed with a case of Monday-itis!

'So happy you could join us, Dr Stevenson,' Hamish snapped, his angry blue eyes meeting hers over his mask.

She took her position on the opposite side of the operating table as the procedure began. They were performing a right knee arthroscopy on Mrs Leonard—a long-time rheumatoid arthritis patient who'd previously had three hip replacements and her left knee replaced, as well as a few knuckle replacements in her hands.

'No happier than I am,' Leesa replied, keeping her tone neutral. 'I did ring through to let you know I'd be running late. It's just been one of those mornings.'

Leesa received no reply to her comments, not even a slight inclination of his head in acknowledgement. Looks as though someone got out on the wrong side of the bed this morning, she thought, but concentrated on the procedure.

Perhaps the good doctor had thought about her too much yesterday. She'd certainly thought about him—and her plan of action. As she'd told him, she was no longer willing to hide her attraction. Not that she was about to make it general knowledge that she was chasing her boss. The admission had been more for Hamish's sake than anyone else's.

'Dr Stevenson,' Hamish said through gritted teeth.

'Yes?' Leesa flicked her eyes away from the small monitor that showed them where their instruments were located. She looked at Hamish, a small smile hidden beneath her mask at his use of her formal title when everyone in the room knew he always called her Leesa.

'Would you mind moving the light a little to the left?'

'Certainly, Hamish. Thank you for mentioning it.' She made sure her voice was cheerful and bright, counterbalancing his grumpy mood.

Deep inside, she was ecstatic at being able to affect him so much but she knew it meant treading more carefully than she had before.

Mrs Leonard's surgery progressed without further reprimand from their head surgeon. Indeed, when they had finished and were de-gowning, their patient stable and on her way to Recovery, Hamish patted her shoulder and commended Leesa on her work.

'At least we finished on time,' Leesa added, still wary of his mood swing.

'Now we can get some lunch and begin clinic on time. Who knows? We may even finish *that* early.' He rubbed his hands together, as though excited about receiving some kind of treat.

When Leesa didn't reply, Hamish merely turned on his heel and headed towards the male changing rooms. Leesa simply watched him walk away, baffled by his behaviour.

Before clinic, Leesa went down to the ward to check in on Mr Lewis as she'd missed the ward round that morning. He was one of her favourite patients as he always had a smile for her. It was now three weeks since his operation and although he was progressing, it was at a slower rate than they'd expected.

'Hello, lass,' he said when she walked into the ward.

One of the other male patients in the ward was Jonno who had been transferred from ICU that morning. As he was currently sleeping, Leesa decided to check his chart after she'd had a chat with Mr Lewis.

'I missed you this morning when Mr O'Donnell did his ward round. Everything all right?'

'Yes and no. I had car trouble and arrived in Theatre quite late.'

'I'll bet *he* wasn't too happy about that.' Mr Lewis chuckled.

'No *he* wasn't but I did ring through to say I'd be late and, short of engaging one of the *Star Trek* transporters, there was nothing else I could do to get here faster. Enough about me. How are you feeling today?'

'I'm starting to get a bit worried, Doc. It's taking me so much longer to recover from this hip replacement than from the last one I had.'

'Mr Lewis, in the past two years since your previous hip replacement you've had two minor strokes with extensive rehabilitation, and this time around you've dislocated your shoulder as well. Your body has had a lot of healing to do and, considering all these factors, it's just taking a little bit longer this time.' She collected his chart from the end of the bed and read the nursing observations. 'Everything is fine, even if it is taking a bit longer than last time.' She returned the chart to its holder and took his left hand in hers. 'I don't want you to start fretting over your progress. Mr O'Donnell is quite satisfied with events so you shouldn't be worrying. *If* there was anything wrong, we'd tell you.'

'Promise?' he asked, his voice barely audible.

'Cross my heart.' Leesa smiled and, after giving his hand a little squeeze, crossed her heart. 'Now, when is Ingrid due in today?'

He sighed. 'She's getting out of work early today but she still won't finish until three o'clock this afternoon.'

'She's a high-school teacher, you said?' Leesa asked, and he nodded.

'We were both teachers but I retired at the end of last year. After the last mini-stroke, it wasn't worth it. I guess I miss being busy, especially when Ingrid is still at it.'

'Relax and enjoy the good life while you can. Smell the roses.'

'Speaking of which,' Denise, the physiotherapist said, walking up to his bed, 'we're about to take a stroll outside.'

'Great. You have fun. I just need to check on your room-mate here…' she indicated Jonno '…before clinic starts.'

'Thanks for stopping by, lass,' Mr Lewis said with a tired smile.

Jonno was still asleep, so Leesa checked his chart before going to the nurses' station to read the nursing notes. Jonno had regained consciousness twenty-four hours after the operation but was suffering from minor amnesia. He knew his name, which turned out to be Herman Johnson—hence the Jonno—and other general things, but regarding the accident he couldn't tell them much. His mind had blanked it out.

His pelvis was supported in a sling and further X-rays had been organised for later that week, even though he was tentatively booked for surgery next Monday morning.

Leesa's beeper sounded and she noted the extension for clinic. She called through.

'Are you planning on running late for everything today, Leesa?' Hamish's voice asked tersely down the line. His bad mood had returned.

'No, Hamish,' she replied. 'I'm on my way.' As she walked to the clinic, stopping to buy a roll from a food-vending machine on the way, she wondered whether her confession about no longer hiding her attraction for Hamish would ultimately make her life worse. If he was going to be constantly grumpy, perhaps she should retract the statement.

Four hours later, as the last patient left her consulting

room, Leesa leaned back in her chair and stretched her arms back over her head.

'All done?' Hamish asked from the doorway, and she quickly dropped her arms, straightening her top. His gaze flicked briefly over her body as he watched her actions.

'Yes.'

'Good. I'll see you tomorrow,' he said with a quick nod of his head. 'Try to be on time.' A small smile tugged at his lips before he quickly hid it.

The good mood had returned. Leesa smiled. She guessed her confession had been worth it after all.

'It's OK to smile when you're happy, Hamish,' she told him. He nodded again, before walking away.

The following Friday, Leesa said goodbye to her last patient for the day. The clinic had run way overtime and it was now almost six-thirty. Sighing, Leesa picked up her pen and began writing up the rest of her notes for the day.

The week had been extremely busy and Hamish had never been more polite in the entire time she'd known him. He'd ensured they'd never been alone together and that the research project they were undertaking had been brought into full-blown operation. This meant a lot of reading as well as interviewing patients who were willing to take part in the research.

It didn't appear that it would slow down any time soon. After all, Leesa *was* his research fellow. Hamish had been successful in obtaining a grant for the twelve-month research fellowship and was required to make certain breakthroughs during that time, so when a detailed report was made at the end of the year it would show strong improvements in the theories he expounded.

Leesa loved the work, loved the pace, but more than anything she wished Hamish would relax and allow them to enjoy it—together!

On Wednesday, Mrs Leonard had been discharged home,

the arthroscopy on her right knee healing well. As Mrs Leonard was a long-time rheumatoid arthritis sufferer, Hamish hoped that the arthroscopy to her knee would delay the need for a total knee replacement but, considering she'd already had both hips replaced as well as her left knee and a few knuckles in her fingers, the right knee was definitely the next in line.

'At least by debriding the knee, as we have, it should buy you a bit more time before we need to replace the knee altogether,' Hamish had told Mrs Leonard on the Wednesday morning ward round before she'd been discharged.

On Thursday, the 3D scans for Jonno's pelvis had indeed indicated that surgical intervention was necessary. The healing to his femur was progressing nicely, while all other injuries were well on their way to recovery.

There was a knock at her consulting-room door, bringing her out of her reverie. She looked up, hoping it wasn't yet another squeezed-in patient.

'Hamish.' She was surprised he'd sought her out, especially as there was no one else in the room.

Leesa put her pen down. 'Please sit down. Whew! What a clinic. I think there should be a law against seeing that many patien—' She stopped as she realised he wasn't listening to her.

He was looking down at her, his face strained as though in agony.

'Leesa,' he whispered, and crossed to her side.

Leesa picked up on his mood. 'Hamish,' she said warily. 'What? What is it?'

She watched as he swallowed, before saying quietly. 'There's been an accident.'

Leesa's eyes widened in anxiety and concern. 'Who? One of our parents?'

He shook his head.

'*Who?*' She tried to stand but Hamish placed a hand on

either shoulder, forcing her to sit. 'Hamish, you're beginning to scare me.'

'It's…Janet and Angus.'

'*What!*' Leesa felt something like a lump of lead in her
heart and tears filled her eyes.

'They were driving back from Moss Vale when a large
wallaby jumped in front of their car. They hit the animal
but it also caused them to swerve out of control and hit a
tree.'

'What…? Where…? Are they…?' She couldn't bring
herself to finish the sentence.

'They're on their way here. The paramedic report was
radioed through and when they learned the patients' iden-
tities, Casualty paged me immediately.'

'When will they arrive?' Leesa stood, impatiently brushing the tears from her face. This time Hamish didn't stop
her from standing and they both headed out of the door.

'In another twenty minutes or so.'

Leesa stopped still in the middle of the corridor. 'Charlotte?' she whispered.

Hamish stopped beside her and grasped her arm, urging
her forward. 'There was no report that she was in the car.
I presume she's still at home with the nanny.'

When they arrived at Casualty, Leesa grabbed the nearest
phone to ring her sister's house. Gabby answered and once
Leesa had checked that everything was all right with
Charlotte, she told Gabby what had happened.

'Can you stay with Charlotte?'

'Of course,' Gabby replied without hesitation.

'I'll come over once I've finished here but I've no idea
what time it will be. I have a key so make sure the house
is locked and secure.'

'Right. I can't believe it,' Gabby said for the umpteenth
time.

'You're not the only one,' Leesa whispered.

'I'll be praying for them,' Gabby said softly.

'Thanks,' Leesa answered, before hanging up. We all will be, she thought as she and Hamish waited impatiently for their siblings to arrive.

CHAPTER FOUR

'STOP pacing up and down, Hamish,' Leesa said wearily. 'You'll wear the carpet out and I doubt if Theatre Sister will thank you for ruining her office.' They'd opted to wait in there for news of both Janet's and Angus's operations as the doctors' tearoom generally had people coming in and out. At least in here they had relative privacy.

'What am I supposed to do?' Hamish thundered. 'You saw the state of them when they were brought into Casualty.'

'Yes, I did, Hamish, and I'm as worried as you are.'

'I could wring Jake's neck for not allowing me into Theatre. That's my brother on that operating table and I want to make sure he gets the *best* treatment there is.' Hamish thumped a fist into his palm.

Leesa placed her empty coffee-cup on the table then sat back against the comfortable cushions of the sofa. 'Hamish,' she sighed.

'What?' He stopped pacing and glared at her with such ferocity that Leesa almost laughed.

'Come and sit down.' She patted the sofa seat beside her. When he didn't move, she ordered, 'Sit!'

Thankfully he didn't argue, because if he had she would have stood and walked out on him. She guessed he probably knew this from her tone of voice—Hamish knew her pretty well.

'Turn around,' she continued to order as he sat stiff and starched on the comfortable cushions.

He exhaled impatiently but again did as she asked. Leesa placed her hands on his shoulders and slowly began to massage.

'You don't need to do this,' he mumbled.

'Yes I do. At least this way I can help you relax. I just need to be doing something—*anything!*'

'I know what you mean.'

Hamish allowed her to continue and after a few minutes of silence Leesa said, 'You know why Jake and Ray wouldn't allow either one of us in Theatre, don't you?'

'Hmph,' Hamish grunted.

'It's against hospital policy to operate on a person you're related to.'

'It is also hospital policy,' Hamish added, 'to have the chief of staff operate on other hospital staff and their next of kin. All I wanted to do was watch.'

'If the positions were reversed and it was Jake's brother in that theatre, there is no way in the world you would have allowed him to stand over your shoulder and watch.'

More mumbling from Hamish.

'Both Jake and Ray are highly qualified and respected orthopaedic surgeons. Next to you and me they're the best, and there's no one I'd rather trust with our siblings than those two.'

'Yeah, you're right,' he conceded.

She could feel Hamish begin to relax slightly and was pleased she'd been able to help him. He carried too much weight on his shoulders, put there by no one but himself. Still, she knew how responsible he felt, not only for Angus but for Janet and herself as well. How could he break the habit of a lifetime?'

'What are you thinking about?' he asked when she'd been silent for a while.

'It's what I'm *not* trying to think about that's occupying my thoughts at the moment. Like when I first saw my sister being wheeled in from the ambulance, unconscious. The way her clothing was torn and dishevelled. The dry and fresh blood around her broken arm and leg. Her hair all

messy and the petrified expression in her eyes when she
briefly regained consciousness.'

Tears began to form in Leesa's eyes. 'Angus looked even
worse and for a moment…I felt my world stand still. Why
does it always do that when things are bad? Why can I
never stop a moment when things are good?'

Leesa began to cry and Hamish quickly turned, envel-
oping her in his arms.

'I know,' he soothed. 'I know exactly how you feel.'

Leesa felt so…cared for, being held in his protective
embrace. She sobbed into his shirt, feeling her tension ebb
away.

'I feel so helpless, Hamish. There's so much I can do to
help my sister yet at the moment all I'm told to do is wait.'

'At least we have each other,' Hamish said. His words
were softly spoken and Leesa gently pulled back from his
embrace. She turned her tear-stained face up to look into
his, knowing she must look a sight with her eyes and nose
all red.

'We *do* have each other,' she agreed. 'You're a great
friend.' Her voice sounded husky and seductive even to her
own ears. They continued to stare at each other, while
Leesa's heart began to hammer wildly against her ribs.

'Leesa,' he whispered, 'I'm trying my hardest to hold
you at arm's length, but the truth is I'm not feeling very
strong at present.'

Her throat went dry as she realised he planned on kissing
her. Without breaking eye contact, she nervously licked her
lips, her breath coming out in heavy gasps as the spiralling
tension within her stomach worked its way to the top.

She didn't want to say anything that would stop the slow,
agonising descent of his mouth to hers. The first kiss. It
was a tremendously important step and one that needed to
work. Leesa was positive that once Hamish had a taste he
wouldn't be able to stop. She wanted him to become ad-
dicted to her—just as she was to him.

At last his lips met hers with an excruciating softness that caused a flood of passion to course throughout her body, leaving her more breathless than before. She could feel her arms begin to tremble as his lips touched hers fleetingly again.

The churning in her stomach picked up speed and Leesa finally knew the sensation of feeling sick with love.

When their lips met for the third time, his tongue caressed her mouth, gently probing its way inside. For a fleeting instant Leesa expected Hamish to pick up the pace immediately. Instead, he took his time, exploring her mouth and allowing her access to his.

Second by second, moment by moment, he raised the level of tension building within her until it reached fever pitch. Now her entire body was trembling with pent-up desire and her breathing was so ragged she would have been surprised at any oxygen reaching her lungs. Her heart was hammering a wild rhythm, its sound reverberating throughout every fibre of her being and deep down in her soul the fire was blazing out of control.

If he'd kissed her with a fierce, hungry passion—as though years of not being able to touch her had caused him to starve—Leesa would have been thrilled. But this…this… sheer torture was intensifying her love. He was so gentle— so caring—so passionately sexy. He was driving her to distraction, and although she wanted him *never* to stop she feared if he didn't she'd soon go into cardiac arrest.

With a superhuman effort Leesa eased slightly back, her eyes closed with fatigue. She felt his fingers and then his thumb caress her swollen lips and another jolt of desire coursed through her.

When he urged her head back to his chest, she didn't resist. He adjusted his position and gathered her closer to him. She was mildly aware of listening to his heartbeat return to normal as her own followed suit. The experience of her first kiss with Hamish had blown all her fantasies out of the water and left her feeling decidedly...sleepy.

'Wake up, sleepyheads.' It was Ray's voice, penetrating the deep sleep Leesa now dragged herself from.

Hamish shot to his feet, leaving her sprawled over the sofa. 'What's the news?'

'Janet is doing well and is about to leave for Recovery. I've called through to Jake in theatre three and he's just closing the wound on Angus's thigh after Grosse and Kempf nailing.' Ray patted Hamish on the back. 'Shouldn't be too much longer now.'

'Right. Thanks,' Hamish said, and, after turning to help Leesa off the sofa, he stalked out of the room.

'It must be hard, having both siblings under the knife at the same time,' Ray commented to Leesa as she gathered up the coffee-cups, knowing Theatre Sister wouldn't appreciate them leaving a mess in her office. 'At least you have each other to help you get through.'

'We're all very close,' Leesa said by way of explaining the sleeping embrace Ray had interrupted. With any luck he'd simply put it down to emotional distress and fatigue.

'I'll deal with these cups. Go and see Janet.'

'Thanks, Ray.' Leesa gave him a quick kiss on the cheek, before handing him the cups. 'Thanks for taking care of my sister.'

Leesa rushed to Recovery where Janet's bed was just being settled. Hamish stood beside the lithe form of her sister like a guard of honour. The recovery nurses were doing their job of settling their patient, working around the towering figure of their head orthopaedic surgeon.

'Make sure she's comfortable. That BP reading can't be right. Take it again,' he was demanding. Leesa tugged on his arm and pulled him to the side.

'Leave them alone, Hamish, or we might be asked to leave.'

'They wouldn't dare,' he said between gritted teeth. 'This is my sister-in-law and—'

'*My sister,*' Leesa added. 'And we'll leave the nurses alone. Bullying them won't help.'

'Thanks, Dr Stevenson,' one of the nurses whispered under her breath, but Hamish had obviously heard as he glared at her.

Leesa stepped back and observed him for a moment. He was more edgy than previously and she wondered whether it had anything to do with that sensual kiss they'd shared and/or being caught sleeping with his research fellow in his arms? She hoped it was both. If Hamish denied the effects that kiss had evoked deep within him, Leesa doubted whether she'd ever forgive him.

When the nurses had finished, both Hamish and Leesa took a quick peek at the external fixator which had been applied to Janet's left tibia, before checking the plaster cast which had been applied to her sister's right arm.

'Her ribs are strapped and apart from whiplash and mild concussion she'll be as good as new once the bruises and scratches start to fade and heal,' Leesa announced to Hamish, a small smile lighting her face.

'Relieved?' he asked, and she nodded. 'Let's hope Angus's prognosis is as good.'

They stayed quietly by Janet's side, moving away in fifteen minutes or so for the nurses to perform their observations. Hamish closely scrutinised the chart once they'd been done, before showing it to Leesa.

'She's doing fine,' he said with a firm hand on her shoulder. 'She'll be just fine.'

'Here comes Angus,' she said as the recovery doors swished open and her brother-in-law was wheeled in, unconscious.

They put his bed next to Janet's. Hamish walked over and simply stood, looking down at his brother. He allowed the nurses to do their work, which surprised Leesa. She'd half expected him to bluster even more than he had for Janet. Although his features were a mask that displayed no emotion, she could tell that the mere sight of Angus in this condition was causing him grief.

One of the nurses handed him the chart. 'We're still waiting for Dr Tindall's notes but he sent a message saying he wanted to discuss things with you.'

Hamish nodded his thanks and flicked through the notes. He turned to Leesa. 'Everything looks all right—for the moment.'

Leesa took the chart from him and had a quick look herself. Jake Tindall had put a Grosse and Kempf nail down Angus's right femur and fixed the fractured collar-bone and scapula with plates and screws. His broken ribs had been securely strapped and a few deep open cuts sutured closed.

'Leesa?' The word was barely audible, but they both heard it. They pivoted to give Janet their attention. Her eyes were still closed. 'I can't lift my arm,' she said softly, her voice scratchy.

'I'll get you some ice chips,' Hamish said, and beckoned to a nurse.

'Your arm is in plaster.'

'Angus?' That was Janet's next question.

'He's here—right beside you and doing fine,' Leesa assured her sister as she bent to kiss her forehead. 'You gave us such a scare,' she whispered as a fresh set of tears began to fill her eyes, 'but you're both going to be just fine.'

'Char—' Janet coughed a little.

'Where are those ice chips?' Hamish mumbled impatiently.

'Charlotte is fine. I've called Gabby and she'll be with Charlotte all night. I'm going to stay there as well when I'm satisfied that you and Angus are sleeping soundly.'

'Thanks.'

'Janet, you don't need to thank me.' Leesa brushed the

tears away impatiently. 'You're my sister. I love you. I'll do anything for you.'

The nurse came with the ice chips and helped Janet have a few while Leesa sniffled and wiped her eyes again. 'You rest now and just get better. Hamish and I will take care of everything.'

'As always,' Janet said, before her breathing settled down into a steady rhythm.

Leesa blew her nose and looked up at Hamish. 'I don't know if I'm strong enough to get through this,' she said, her lower lip quivering.

Hamish immediately enveloped her in his arms. His action surprised and elated Leesa. Hamish always kept his professional image in place at the hospital yet here he was hugging her in the middle of Recovery, but she also knew that the grapevine would simply portray him as a caring surrogate brother.

For a man who rarely showed any emotion there were a few cracks beginning to appear in the brick wall he'd built around himself. Although she hadn't anticipated it happening this way—at the expense of their siblings—Leesa was thrilled it was happening, nevertheless.

Someone tapped Hamish on the shoulder and they both turned around to find Jake standing there, Angus's case-notes in his hands.

'Everything all right?' he asked with genuine concern.

'Janet's just regained consciousness,' Leesa explained as she sniffed again.

'May I?' Hamish asked, and held out his hand for the notes.

'Be my guest. Everything went according to plan, with the only complication being a mix up in CDs. I could have sworn my Mozart CD was in my briefcase, yet when I sent someone to check they only found my Bach CD.'

Leesa smiled. 'Glad to hear that was the only complication.'

'In time,' Jake added, 'there's no reason why he can't make a complete and uneventful recovery.'

'That's the best news I've heard all evening,' Leesa said, and turned to hug Jake. It wasn't something she usually did—hug her colleagues—but, then, these circumstances weren't exactly normal.

Jake seemed a bit surprised but returned the embrace all the same.

'Thank you,' Leesa said as she stepped back. 'Both you and Ray have been fantastic.'

Hamish held out his hand to Jake. 'Sorry about before. About yelling at you when you wouldn't let me watch the operation,' he clarified.

Jake shook his hand. 'Don't mention it. If the positions had been reversed, I would have wanted to be there for my family, too. My work here is done so I'll see you both tomorrow morning for ward round.'

Both Leesa and Hamish stayed in Recovery until Angus regained consciousness.

'Janet?' he asked before his eyes were open.

'She's right here, mate. Right beside you,' Hamish said calmly. Angus opened his eyes. 'You've been in Theatre for a while,' Hamish said, reading the unspoken query in his brother's eyes. 'But you're going to be just fine and so is Janet,' he added forcefully.

'Hi, gorgeous,' Leesa whispered as she came around to the other side of the bed and kissed Angus on the forehead. 'I've called Gabby and she'll stay with Charlotte. As soon as you're both transferred to the ward, I'll go back to your house and live there until things settle down.'

'You go, too,' Angus croaked, his voice dry and raspy. His words were directed at Hamish. 'Leesa and Charlotte need you, Hamish. More than ever.'

Hamish looked at Leesa, their gazes locking for a moment. Leesa held her breath, waiting nervously for his response.

'Leesa's a big girl now, Angus. She doesn't need me looking over her shoulder.'

Leesa didn't know whether to be overjoyed or offended by his words. Clearly he was trying to avoid spending time alone with her in that big house, and Leesa found that complimentary. His statement to Angus also implied he was acknowledging that she'd grown up and didn't require his surrogate brother act any more. Although, now that it wasn't available, she instantly started to miss it.

'For me?' Angus said, and again Leesa was sure there was silent communication passing between the two brothers that she didn't understand.

'Just rest now,' Hamish prompted, and Angus did as his brother suggested.

Leesa and Hamish watched as the nurses diligently performed their observations before they read the charts again.

'Janet's improving considerably. They'll probably move her to the ward soon.'

'Angus will go to ICU.'

'Why?' Leesa took the chart off Hamish. 'So there are a few "watch" areas noted down. That's normal.'

'Maybe so, but Jake's requested he go to ICU and I agree. If there are any nasty surprises waiting to happen, I'd much prefer him to be in ICU where he's receiving specialised treatment. It's just for the next twenty-four hours.'

They were both silent for a while, watching their siblings as they slept peacefully. 'Don't feel obliged to stay until they're both settled for the night,' Hamish said eventually. 'I can stay and you can go and check up on Charlotte.'

Why was he acting so weird all of a sudden? 'Thanks, but I'd rather wait until I know they're both stable and comfortable for the night. Gabby's with Charlotte who by now will be fast asleep.'

Hamish shrugged. 'Suit yourself,' he replied noncommittally.

It was another fifteen minutes before the nurses were satisfied with Janet's progress and ready to move her to the ward. Leesa went with the bed, holding her sister's hand while Hamish stayed with Angus in Recovery.

'Do I look as bad as I feel?' Janet asked with a drowsy smile once she was settled.

'Probably worse.'

'Gee, thanks.'

'I'm only telling you the truth. You have quite a few awful bruises and they always look worse than they really are.'

'Thanks for being here,' Janet said.

'We went through this in Recovery,' Leesa remarked with a smile as she pushed Janet's hair back from her forehead.

'Did we? I don't remember.'

'That's common. We talked about Angus and the fact that he's fine. We talked about Charlotte and how Gabby and I will take care of her.'

'Charlotte.' Tears sprang instantly to Janet's eyes. 'Oh, my baby. I'm so thankful she wasn't in the car with us.'

'True,' Leesa replied, not wanting to even think about what might have been.

'Bring her in soon. I miss her like crazy already.'

'I promise to bring her in tomorrow. Little girl cuddle-and-kiss therapy will be very good for both her parents.'

Janet smiled at the thought and closed her eyes again.

'You rest now, Janet. I'm going to check on Angus and then I think I'll head back to your house. I'll pack some things for both of you and bring them in tomorrow as well.'

'Mmm,' Janet replied as she drifted back off to sleep.

When Leesa returned to Recovery, the nurses there informed her Angus had just been taken to ICU.

'Mr O'Donnell, of course, was in tow. He's taken it pretty hard, hasn't he?' one of the nurses asked.

Leesa smiled, knowing what the other woman was get-

ting at. 'I guess when you see him being so aloof and professional all the time, it's hard to believe he's a real person
with real feelings and a real family to care for.'

'I guess you're right. This was the man not the director
of orthopaedics who was here tonight,' the nurse agreed.
'Perhaps also because he's a man we don't expect him to
be vulnerable, like we females.'

'You may have a point,' Leesa agreed, not wanting to
stay and chat but also not wanting to appear rude. 'I'll just
nick down to ICU and say goodnight. Thanks for everything, by the way.'

'No worries,' the nurse replied before Leesa headed out
the door.

Hamish left her alone to speak with Angus when she
arrived in ICU. She promised him as well that she'd bring
Charlotte around to visit tomorrow.

'Just get better, please,' she asked. 'I need my brother
and my sister in one hundred per cent health before my
world will right itself again.'

She went to the nurses' station but found no sign of
Hamish.

'He's in the sister's office,' the night registrar informed
her.

Leesa went across the hall soundlessly, used to walking
quietly through a hospital at night-time. She knocked on
the door and entered without waiting for a reply. Hamish
was sitting down, his mobile phone at his ear.

'They'll both make a complete recovery.'

Leesa knew instinctively that he was talking to his parents.

'No. In my opinion, you don't need to come back to
Australia, but if it will put your minds at rest then by all
means do so. I don't want you to think you're not wanted—
quite the contrary.'

Another pause. 'If you were heading this way at the end
of the month, then wait until then. Both of them will be in

hospital for at least two to four weeks, and when they do go home *that's* when they'll be needing the help. You know, cooking, cleaning—that type of thing.'

He listened to his mother again. 'I called Karen earlier. You remember, she's Janet's and Angus's secretary/receptionist, so she'll organise their patients and locums.' Pause. 'Yes, she's here. She's on her way back to stay with Charlotte and the nanny for the night. Sure.' He held out the phone. 'My mother would like a word.'

'Hi, Mary,' Leesa said into Hamish's small mobile phone.

'Oh, darling, how are you holding up?'

'Just fine. Janet's all settled for the night and so is Angus. They're both going to be fine.'

'So Hamish has told me. Leesa, I want you to make sure that Hamish doesn't overdo things. You know how he tends to carry the burden of the entire world on his shoulders and appears to be coping?'

'Do I ever.'

'Appearances can be deceiving. Look after him, dear.'

'I have been,' Leesa replied, trying not to give too much away with Hamish standing right beside her, listening to every word she said. Mary O'Donnell was Leesa's biggest fan when it came to helping Hamish realise his surrogate sister had grown up.

'That's good to hear,' Mary said meaningfully. 'Keep it up.'

'So we'll see you at the end of March, as originally planned?'

'Yes. Hamish seems to think it's best and we all know he's hardly ever wrong.'

Leesa smiled. 'See you then. Give my love to Mum and Dad—oh, and Sean, too.'

'Will do, dear. Kiss our beautiful Charlotte for her grandparents. Bye.'

Leesa handed the phone back to Hamish who quickly

finished the call. He leaned back in the chair and ran a hand through his hair.

'Janet settled?'

'She's sleeping soundly.'

'Angus is ready for his night-time medication, so once he's had that I'll follow you back to their place.'

Leesa's eyes widened. 'You're going to stay, too?'

'It's what Angus wants,' Hamish replied.

'What do *you* want, Hamish?'

'I want to keep my brother's and sister-in-law's stress down to a minimum. If that means both you and I—and the nanny—live at their house full time until their return, caring for our niece, then that's what happens.'

'You don't think it might be just a little bit too close for comfort?'

'Meaning?' She could tell he was unsettled by the way he stood and started pacing up and down the room.

'Well, that kiss before was pretty powerful.'

He raked his hand through his hair again. 'Hmm. I guess we should talk.'

'No,' Leesa replied. 'I'm going back to my place to pick up a few things then I'll go to Janet's and Angus's. After that I'll be getting some sleep so that in the morning I can spend time with my niece after I've brought her to the hospital to see her parents and done a ward round. What I don't need is a post-morten on the most incredible kiss I've ever had in my entire life. Waiting for our siblings to come out of Theatre may have intensified the emotions we were both feeling, but it's no reason to make excuses or offer analysis on why it happened. It *did* happen, Hamish, and whether you like it or not it was...*incredible*.'

He was silent when she finished her spiel. 'Well?' she prompted.

He shook his head. 'You've said all that needed to be said,' he replied. 'I'll swing by my place as well and meet you at their house.'

'Oh.' Leesa frowned. She'd expected him to say some-thing more regarding the new direction their relationship was taking. 'Fine. OK, I'll see you there.' She turned and headed for the door.

'Leesa,' he said softly, and she turned around. In a few short strides he was beside her. He lowered his head and kissed her briefly on the lips. 'My mother said I should stop taking you for granted—so thank you.'

Leesa was astonished. 'For what?' she asked, a little dazed by his action.

'For being there for me during the afternoon. It was a...' He hesitated. 'A difficult time.'

'Yes, it was. Thanks for being there for me, too.' She stood on tiptoe and kissed him the same way he'd kissed her. When she'd finished, he did something else that sur-prised her.

He groaned and gathered her close. He didn't make any further attempt to kiss her but instead seemed content sim-ply to hold her in his arms. They stood there for a good five minutes, Leesa relaxing against his strong and familiar frame.

Eventually he put her from him.

'These next few weeks are going to be hard.' His tone was brisk yet husky, his eyes filled with desire.

'Let's just take things one small step at a time,' Leesa suggested.

'Good idea.' Hamish nodded. 'Let's go.'

They checked on Angus before Hamish walked Leesa to her car. He bent his head again and kissed her lips fleet-ingly—as though if he stayed too long, he'd never want to give them up.

'Drive carefully,' he insisted. 'I'll see you there.'

He shut her car door and Leesa started the engine. 'Oh, you'll see me all right,' she murmured as she drove out of the hospital car park, a huge smile on her face. 'By the time our siblings arrive home from hospital, Hamish, my darling, you won't know what has hit you.'

CHAPTER FIVE

GABBY was still awake when they both arrived at Janet's and Angus's house. 'It's almost eleven o'clock,' Leesa said. 'You should have gone to bed.'

'I wouldn't have been able to sleep,' Gabby said. 'Even after you called and told me they were both fine, I still wanted to wait up for you.'

'I don't believe we've been formally introduced,' Hamish said, and extended a hand to Gabby.

'Sorry.' Leesa apologised. 'It's late and it's been one hectic afternoon.'

'Don't apologise,' Gabby insisted. 'Will you be staying, too, Hamish?' she asked, trying to smother a yawn.

'Yes. This family sticks together.'

'Good to hear,' Gabby replied.

'Everything OK with Charlotte?' Leesa asked, anxious for her niece.

'She was a bit unsettled going to sleep but that's to be expected. I believe Angus usually puts her to bed, and anything that breaks their normal routine usually causes slight upsets.'

'That's true. I'll check on her before I turn in.'

'Well…' Gabby yawned again. 'I guess you two know where everything is so I'll head on up to bed.' She turned to leave before remembering something. 'I've changed the sheets on their bed so you could sleep there, Leesa. Sorry, Hamish. If I'd known you were coming, I could have made up one of the other beds for you.'

'Don't worry about it,' Hamish said with a shake of his head. 'I'll be fine. Thanks for everything, Gabby. It was a relief to everyone that you were here with Charlotte this evening.'

'I second that, as do Janet and Angus.'

'Glad I could help,' the young nanny replied. 'Good-night.'

When she'd gone, Leesa turned to Hamish. 'I don't know about you but I've just realised I'm a bit hungry.'

'What are you suggesting?'

'We're in my sister's house and she's a brilliant cook. What do you say we check out the contents of her fridge and cupboards to see what we can come up with?'

Without waiting for an answer, she went into the kitchen and opened the fridge, before checking the freezer.

'Mmm—lasagne. In individual-sized portions—just what the doctor ordered. How about you?'

'Sure. You won't…you know…wreck it just by defrost-ing it, will you?'

Leesa detected the small smile twitching at the corners of Hamish's lips. 'No, I won't,' she said, pretending to be offended. 'My cooking—or, rather, my defrosting—isn't that bad. I must say, Hamish, it is nice to see your sense of humour surface after everything that's happened.'

'Everything meaning the car accident or what happened between you and I?'

Leesa shrugged while she continued to prepare the la-sagne for the microwave. 'Take your pick.'

He didn't reply but instead switched the kettle on for a cup of tea. Janet's kitchen was fairly decent in size but when Hamish entered it to make the tea, Leesa suddenly began to feel claustrophobic. The microwave beeped and she opened the door to test the food, her elbow banging into Hamish as he collected the teabags.

'Sorry,' she mumbled, and realised the butterflies had returned to her stomach.

They continued with their preparations in silence and

soon they were perched on stools on opposite sides of the bench.

'Delicious, as usual,' Hamish murmured after the first mouthful. 'Why is it that you didn't receive the cooking gene as well?'

'It didn't seem fair that I should receive *all* the best talents. Janet was entitled to at least one.'

Hamish laughed. 'Are you trying to sell me a package deal?'

'If I could cook—' Leesa's eyes were alive with mischief '—would you accept this package?'

The humour disappeared from Hamish's face and he looked into her eyes. 'Leesa.' He put his fork down and took her hand in his. 'I can't pretend I don't have feelings for you but there are more things to take into consideration than just our feelings.'

'I realise that,' Leesa responded. 'Just hearing you admit you have feelings for me is enough—that and a few more of those delicious kisses.'

Hamish smiled again and released her hand. 'Do you think that's a good idea?' he asked as they continued to eat.

'To begin with. The fact that you're still trying to keep me at arm's length means I'm doing something right.'

'If I were to give you advice about a relationship between the two of us, it would be to stop flirting with me.'

'I'm not flirting,' she protested with mock innocence.

'Oh, no?' His eyebrows shot up disbelievingly. 'Well, whatever you choose to call it—stop it.'

'Why?'

'Because it's working,' he grumbled good-naturedly.

'Good.'

'Leesa!' he said with a hint of exasperation.

'Hamish,' she replied. She ate the last mouthful then cleared away the plates and stacked them in the dishwasher.

'If we're going to be living in the same house, as well

as working together,' he said, his gaze never leaving her,
'I feel we need a few more ground rules.'

'So you're really worried you won't be able to keep your
hands off me.'

'Leesa!'

'Sorry. Continue.'

'We need to focus on what's important, and at the moment it's Janet's and Angus's recovery and little Charlotte.'

'Agreed.'

'We've moved in here to help maintain a somewhat stable influence in her life so, to that end, I'll see if I can get
some of our on-call shifts covered—at least for the next
few weeks.'

'Good idea.'

'I think we need to be mature and adult about this.'

'Living together, you mean?'

'Yes.'

'Absolutely.' Leesa stood up and came around to his side
of the bench, swishing her hips provocatively. 'We'll be
just like brother…' she kissed one cheek '…and sister.' She
kissed the other cheek. 'Goodnight, Hamish.' She pressed
her lips to his firmly and took advantage of his shock to
slip her tongue between his lips. Before he could gather
her close or deepen the kiss, she pulled away.

'Sleep well…bro!'

Around three a.m., Leesa was woken by Charlotte's cries.
She quickly slipped out of bed and rushed into the baby's
room. Gabby was holding her and pacing up and down.

'Is she all right?' Leesa asked, placing a concerned hand
on her niece's forehead.

'I've given her teething gel and some infant paracetamol
but she still won't stop crying.'

'I'll take her,' Leesa said, and reached for the little
munchkin she loved so dearly.

'You're sure?'

'Yes. Go and get some more sleep. You look dead on your feet.'

'What about you?'

'I'm used to being up all hours,' Leesa said with a sleepy smile. 'Not with babies but with emergencies.'

'OK. See you *later* in the morning.'

'Hey, gorgeous,' Leesa crooned as little Charlotte's whimpering stopped for a moment. Leesa's blue eyes met those of her blue-eyed niece. 'Hello, my little darling. Aunty Leesa's here and everything is going to be just fine. Shh,' she whispered.

Charlotte gurgled and, like a rainbow after a shower, a beautiful smile appeared. 'I love you, too, sweetheart,' Leesa told her. Charlotte began to giggle and Leesa shook her head. 'No, it's not playtime, it's still sleep-time. If the sun isn't awake, you shouldn't be either.'

'Need any help?' Hamish's deep voice said softly from the open doorway.

Leesa looked up to see him leaning against the door-frame, wearing only a pair of pyjama bottoms which she guessed had only been added for the benefit of a household of women.

'She's fine now. Although Gabby's been with her during the day, hers is still not a face she's too familiar with yet. At least she's stopped crying but now the gorgeous little miss thinks she's going to play.'

'Medication?' he asked, still standing in the doorway. It was as though he wanted to maintain his distance. Leesa couldn't blame him. He looked so cuddly and lovable wearing basically nothing, with his hair tousled from the pillow.

'Gabby gave her teething gel and paracetamol. If her teeth were the problem, the medicine's now working because she's quite happy. So Uncle Hamish may as well go back to bed. Isn't that right, my darling?' she asked her niece.

'Right. I guess that's just what I'll do.'

When he didn't move, Leesa looked at him with curiosity. 'Next time,' he said, his voice strangely strained, 'try and put something over that flimsy piece of material you probably call a nightie.'

The lace-trimmed satin nightie was as creamy as her skin and came quite high up on her thigh. She'd made it as a present to herself when she'd been accepted for the research fellowship, only dreaming that Hamish might one day see it—but not when she was holding a baby.

'I was in a hurry but thank you for pointing it out, Hamish. I'll make every attempt to remember.'

'Good,' he mumbled, the desire in his eyes unmistakable. When he'd gone, Leesa looked down at her niece.

'Well, Charlotte, I guess I should thank you for waking up and helping in my campaign to change Uncle Hamish's perception of me.'

Charlotte gurgled and kicked her little legs.

'Come on, little miss. I think you can come and cuddle Aunty Leesa for the rest of the morning.' She changed Charlotte's wet nappy, hoping to afford her a bit more comfort, before she returned to her room.

Charlotte snuggled right against Leesa and closed her eyes almost instantly, as though to say, All I wanted was a cuddle.

'Oh, little girl,' Leesa whispered. 'You could become so very addictive.' She kissed the small head that was beside her on the pillow and closed her own eyes, slipping back into dreamland.

That was how Hamish found them the next morning. When Leesa hadn't surfaced by seven a.m., Hamish went in search of her. He'd half expected little Charlotte to be up at the crack of dawn before he remembered that she had. Not exactly dawn but still early enough.

He stood by the bed—the one his brother shared with

his wife—looking down at two of the women who were so important in his life. His little niece and his surrogate sister.

The vision of Leesa standing there, her blonde hair all messy, holding a gorgeous baby and wearing a small piece of material that was actually called clothing, had driven him almost to distraction. If she'd been trying to get the message across to him that she was no longer a child—a teenager who needed his protection—nothing could have achieved it any better than the sight of her last night.

When he'd returned to his room, he'd been unable to get back to sleep. Instead, he'd phoned the hospital to check on Janet's and Angus's condition, before pacing around his room countless times.

He'd imagined what it would be like to come home to that sight every night. To see Leesa—his wife—holding their baby lovingly in her arms. The thought had sent such a powerful blow to his solar plexus he'd actually had to concentrate on his breathing to help it return to normal.

While he stood there, looking down at them, Charlotte's eyes snapped open. She looked at him before a smile appeared on her face. Her little legs started moving and she held out her arms.

Being careful not to wake Leesa, Hamish picked up his niece and crept out of the room.

'Let's let Aunty Leesa have a bit more sleep,' he told his niece as they made their way into the kitchen. 'Now, what can Uncle Hamish get you for breakfast?'

Leesa stretched languorously and settled back under the covers, trying to figure out what day it was and whether she was allowed to enjoy the luxury of a few more minutes in bed before her alarm clock woke her up.

Slowly her mind began to slip from the haze slumber had produced and she opened her eyes. This wasn't her room.

'Charlotte!' The name sprang from her lips as she sat

bolt upright in bed and lifted the covers, looking for her niece. She looked at the door. It was shut. She was sure she'd left it open after bringing Charlotte in earlier.

'Hamish.' She nodded in conclusion and climbed out of bed, collecting the matching robe to her nightie before she walked to the door. She put it on and had tied the belt at her waist before she reached the kitchen.

'Hi!' Hamish said, upon seeing her. He stood before Charlotte's high chair with a bowl of what she presumed to be cereal in one hand and a spoon in the other. 'Here's Aunty Sleepyhead,' he told Charlotte.

'You could have woken me,' Leesa protested. 'Where's Gabby?'

'She's gone home to collect some more clothes and her university books since she'll be living here for the next few days. She'll be back later this afternoon.'

She watched as his gaze scanned her attire and after the brief inspection was surprised to feel the now familiar warmth flood through her, causing colour to flush her cheeks.

'Oh,' she replied after a moment. Leesa felt a little self-conscious, standing there in the kitchen wearing her nightie *and* robe but still feeling under-dressed with Hamish dressed in comfortable jeans and a polo shirt.

She'd wanted Hamish to see her dressed in flimsy lingerie during the evening but not necessarily in the bright light of day in the middle of her sister's kitchen while her niece was having breakfast!

'I thought I told you to put a robe over…that.' His tone was gruff as he sneaked another quick look at her before diverting his gaze back to Charlotte.

'This *is* the robe,' she informed him.

'Really?' He cleared his throat and put another spoonful of breakfast into Charlotte's mouth. 'Remind me to buy you what *I* think constitutes a robe.'

Leesa was temporarily at a loss for words. She was *really*

having an effect on Hamish. Everything she'd ever dreamed of was beginning to happen and now she wasn't at all sure how to handle it. 'If everything's fine here, I'll go take a shower and get dressed.'

'Good idea,' she heard him murmur as she turned and walked out. It wasn't until Leesa was under the spray in the shower that she remembered she'd forgotten to ask after Janet and Angus. She knew Hamish would have been in contact with the hospital. He must think she was dreadful, not even asking after her family.

She made sure it was the first question on her lips when she returned to the kitchen dressed in denim shorts and a white cotton T-shirt. Being the beginning of March, the weather was still quite hot.

The kitchen was deserted and she casually strolled through the house before she realised that both Hamish and Charlotte had done another disappearing act. She called out but received no answer. She decided to check the back yard and here she found Hamish crawling around on the grass with his niece, chasing a bright orange ball that had a tinkling bell inside.

Leesa's heart warmed at the sight and it had nothing to do with the brilliant sunshine. It had everything to do with the man she'd once termed 'unemotional'. The wall he'd secured around himself was beginning to crumble. She also knew he probably didn't like it.

The feelings of desire and passion he'd displayed towards her had to be causing such havoc within him, as though his worst enemy were himself. The accident yesterday had only caused a few more pieces to fall from the wall and here was little Charlotte, breaking down yet another section.

'There you two are,' she called as she walked over to them. Charlotte carefully stood up by herself and held her arms out to her aunty. 'You are a clever little thing to stand up by yourself,' Leesa praised her. 'Before long, you'll be into everything and creating more havoc than you do now.'

'Just like her aunty,' Hamish added as he slowly stood.

Leesa watched the way his gaze travelled the length of her legs as he straightened, and when they met her own gaze he gave her a teasing smile.

'Would you like to take a picture? It would last longer.'

'Why take a picture when I can look at the real person?' he asked with a raised eyebrow.

'Why, indeed?' she responded with a happy smile, both surprised and pleased with his answer. Definitely thawing!

Charlotte clapped her hands, as though bringing them both back to attention—her attention.

'If you would like to have some breakfast, we'll head off to the hospital,' Hamish announced.

'Of course.' Leesa quickly took Charlotte inside, cross with herself for once again forgetting to ask after her family. How could he do it? How could Hamish make her forget all rational thought? Surely she was used to his personality, his mere presence, by now. They'd been friends for…well, for ever yet he still managed to affect her way too much.

'How are they both this morning?' She put Charlotte down on the carpet with her toys and made some toast. 'Tea?' she asked as she switched the kettle on.

'Yes, please. They're both fine. Angus was moved to the ward late last night. I've arranged for them both to be transferred into a private ward together after Jake and Ray have seen them.'

'Considerate to the last.'

'I am the director of the department. Why can't I pull a few strings now and then?'

'Exactly,' Leesa agreed. She made the tea and ate her toast, ensuring that Hamish had eaten as well.

'Charlotte helped me eat my breakfast as well as hers. I

can hardly believe that someone so little can put away so much food.'

'She's a growing girl.' Leesa watched her niece playing contentedly with her toys.

'You *really* love her, don't you.' It was a statement Hamish had made, and Leesa nodded, tears instantly forming in her eyes.

'I love children and since she's my one and only niece I absolutely adore her. I think the only other children I could possibly love more will be my own.'

'How many would you like to have?'

It took her a split second to realise he wasn't proposing or offering to have them with her. He was just making a general enquiry.

'At least two—maybe more. I think it's important for children to have siblings, if possible. Janet and I are the best of friends and have always been close. I wouldn't want my children to miss out on that same bond.'

'I agree. Yesterday only reinforced that bond.' He gave a humourless laugh. 'To think that Angus roamed the globe, working under cover for that pharmaceutical company for years. *Anything* could have happened to him—but didn't. Yet, lo and behold, once he's happily married with a child and has settled down, he's in a car accident.'

'He'll be fine.'

'I know he will. It's just the irony of the situation.'

'We need to live each day as though it were our last.' Leesa looked at him and he at her. His hand came across the bench and closed over her own.

Neither one of them spoke. Instead, the moment seemed to stand still. A good moment!

'We'd better get going,' he said as he drained his cup. 'Do we need to take anything for Charlotte?'

'Yes. I'll pack a bag with some food and drink and extra nappies for her.' Leesa stopped loading the dishwasher and turned to Hamish. 'What about her car seat? Was it in the car when they crashed?'

Hamish smiled. 'Thankfully not. I found it by the back door and Gabby gave me the safety bolt, that's required by law, from her car.'

Leesa released the breath she was holding. 'Good. Well, then, I'll pack the bag. Would you mind checking to see if Charlotte is still clean?'

'Of course she's clean.' He pointed to the child dressed in a pretty pink dress, with frilly socks and soft pink booties. 'Gabby only dressed her about an hour ago and she's been happily playing outside—' He stopped in mid-sentence. 'You mean check her nappy, don't you?'

Leesa nodded, her eyes twinkling with merriment. 'Have you ever changed a nappy, Hamish?'

'Can't say that I have.' He was now eyeing Charlotte suspiciously.

'Amazing!' Leesa zipped up the baby-bag and crossed to pick up Charlotte. 'There is actually something in this world that Uncle Hamish has never done.'

'I can change that.'

'Your stubborn pride serves you well,' Leesa remarked after she'd checked Charlotte's nappy. 'She's dirty and she's all yours. I'll get the things I need, bolt in her car seat and pack everything in your car. Call me if you need help.

With that, Leesa handed him his niece and walked out. Once everything was in the car, she walked to the nursery. 'How are things progressing?' The smile on her face was instant and a bubble of laughter escaped.

Hamish's face was wrinkled in absolute agony at the smell as he begged Charlotte to keep her legs and arms still so he could complete the change.

'How could someone so small and gorgeous make such a hideous mess?' he asked as he caught hold of one of her kicking legs and then the other. Leesa couldn't help herself and roared with laughter. Indignant, Hamish continued to clean Charlotte and was finally able to attach the clean nappy.

Leesa's laughter simmered down and she wiped the tears from her eyes. 'Why don't you go and wash your hands?' she offered, taking pity on him. 'I'll finish dressing her.'

Hamish fled from the room and Leesa turned to her niece. 'Give me a high five,' she joked with a beaming smile and caught Charlotte's hand in hers. 'Between us, we'll get Uncle Hamish into line.'

They found him waiting by the car, his composure returned. 'Your chariot, my ladies.' He opened the rear door with a sweeping gesture and Leesa secured Charlotte into her car seat.

Hamish locked the house, setting the alarm, and returned to the car. When he was seated Leesa leaned over and kissed his cheek. 'You did well, Uncle Hamish.'

He shuddered but gave her a smile. 'I'll get better.'

'That's the spirit.' She laughed again. 'I can't wait to tell your brother. It will really cheer him up.'

When they arrived at the hospital Charlotte received all the attention. As they walked to the ward people smiled and waved to her. Other staff members simply stared at the sight of Hamish and Leesa, walking through the hospital with a baby.

She was sure by now that the grapevine had once again done its job and everyone would know about the accident in which their siblings had been involved.

'My darling.' The smile on Janet's face was beaming as she held out her good arm to her baby girl. Charlotte wriggled impatiently in Leesa's arms and almost threw herself onto Janet.

'Mumumumum,' she gurgled with delight and buried her little face in Janet's shoulder.

'Ugh,' Janet groaned. 'Careful, darling. Mummy's a bit sore.'

Leesa watched as Janet kissed her daughter's head, tears forming in her eyes. 'I've missed you so much, my baby. Mummy loves you.'

Tears began to prick behind Leesa's eyes, too, and she walked over to Angus who was talking to Hamish. 'Good morning, brother-in-law.' She kissed him. 'You're... looking slightly better than yesterday but still not too good. Are you feeling pain anywhere?'

'I've just had the third degree from big brother here. With all the breaks and bruises I have scattered around my body, surely I'm bound to feel *some* pain?'

'The analgesics should be taking care of it,' Hamish answered, and reached immediately for his brother's chart.

'Stop worrying, both of you, and see if you can prise Charlotte off Janet long enough for me to have a kiss and cuddle.'

'With Janet or Charlotte?' Leesa asked, and Angus glared at her.

'I'd love to have both, but at the moment I'll have to be content simply to hold my wife's hand.'

Leesa lifted Charlotte from Janet and took her over to Angus.

'Last night,' Janet said, her eyes beginning to close, 'when they brought Angus down, the nurses kindly pushed our beds closer together so we could hold hands. They said they'd had strict orders from the director of orthopaedics to do anything, within reason, to make us completely comfortable.'

Hamish shrugged. 'It's the least I could do.'

'Thank you, Hamish.' Janet's eyes remained closed and her words were a whisper.

Charlotte was now wanting to crawl all over her father's bed so Leesa picked her up. 'Why don't we find some bread and feed the ducks?' she asked Charlotte. 'Mummy and Daddy are going to have a little sleep but we'll come back and see them later.'

'Mumumumum,' Charlotte said with a frown, her voice starting to rise. She held out her arms to her sleeping mother.

'I know it's hard, darling,' Angus said. 'You go with Aunty Leesa and we'll see you soon.'

'No,' Charlotte squealed.

'We'll go before she upsets the ward. She'll be fine, Angus,' Leesa assured him.

'I'm not worried.' He yawned. 'She's in the best of care.'

'I'll stay,' Hamish told Leesa, and she nodded, taking Charlotte out before she erupted into a tantrum.

'It's not easy, is it, darling?' Leesa crooned as she held the child close to her. 'They'll be better soon.'

'Mumumumum,' Charlotte sobbed into Leesa's shoulder.

'Let's meet some new people, find some bread and feed those ducks,' Leesa suggested, and silently thanked whatever committee had long ago built a little pond, complete with ducks, at the rear of the hospital grounds.

She took Charlotte into the men's ward and introduced her to Mr Lewis. Her crying soon subsided and as the centre of attention again, she was happy.

'Isn't she a darling?' he said as he tickled Charlotte under her chin. She wasn't a child who usually went to strangers but Mr Lewis was an instant hit. Charlotte giggled and smiled for him, uplifting his heart and making his day.

'How are your sister and her husband doing?' Mr Lewis asked softly, a smile still on his face for Charlotte's benefit.

'They'll be fine—in time.'

'Oh, yes, time is a great healer—for *all* wounds.' He tickled Charlotte again and was rewarded with another giggle. 'Her laughter is infectious. I think you should record it and play it over a loudspeaker. That'll help a few of the people in here.'

Leesa smiled. 'She usually doesn't take to strangers but you're wrapped around her little finger.'

'I'll bet I'm not the only one,' he said with a chuckle.

'Without sounding modest, I have a way with kids. It's the reason I became a teacher.' His tone held a wistful note and Leesa could tell he clearly missed his work.

'Is she walking yet?'

'Almost. Pulling herself up on furniture—that sort of thing.'

'So you and Mr O'Donnell will be babysitting until your siblings are well enough for discharge?'

'Yes. Janet, my sister, has employed a nanny who'll be staying in the house as well, then once they're ready for discharge both sets of parents should be home from overseas and can take over.'

'Sounds as though it's all been neatly planned out.'

'Yes, it has.'

'It's wonderful that you and Mr O'Donnell are there to help your families out. It's rare in this day and age.'

'It's the least we can do for the people we love.'

Charlotte began to squirm even more in Leesa's arms, wanting to get onto Mr Lewis's bed, but, considering his injuries, there was no way her aunt was giving in to her.

'We're on our way out to feed the ducks—after we find some bread.'

'If I weren't due for another physio treatment, I'd join you myself. Have fun. Bye-bye, Charlotte.' He waved. 'Come and visit me again some time.'

Charlotte gurgled and clapped her hands, her beaming smile still firmly in place.

They spent the next fifteen minutes meeting every member of staff between the ward and the cafeteria.

'You're certainly a fast worker, Leesa,' Caroline Metcalfe said from behind them. Leesa turned around.

'Hi. Meet my niece, Charlotte.'

'Hello. Aren't you a gorgeous one? She looks a lot like her uncle...*and* you. In fact, she could pass for your daughter.'

'Scary, isn't it?' Leesa covered the lump which had in-stantly formed in her throat with a laugh. If only!

'I was sorry to hear about your sister and her husband. How are they progressing?'

'Fair. Angus still doesn't look right so Hamish has stayed with him. They'll both recover—in time.'

'And where are the two of you off to?'

'We're going to get some bread to feed the ducks, aren't we, Charlotte?'

Charlotte didn't respond but simply buried her head shyly into Leesa's shoulder.

'Have fun. I'm off to Theatre for a mop-up list.

'I didn't think you worked weekends?'

'I'm covering for a sick staff member.' She rolled her eyes and shrugged. 'What can you do?' She paid for her ice-coffee milk and looked at her watch. 'In fact, I'd better get going or I'll be late. Bye.'

'Wave bye-bye, Charlotte,' Leesa suggested, and was pleased and surprised when Charlotte did just that. 'Now, let's get that bread and feed those ducks.'

They had a lovely time feeding the ducks—or rather Leesa did—sitting down on the grass and throwing bread to them. Charlotte was more than content to crawl on the grass, hoping to catch one, but the ducks were far too quick.

'Never mind, blossom,' Leesa said, and handed her some bread. Instead of throwing it, Charlotte went to put it in her mouth. 'No, Charlotte. Throw it for the ducks to eat.' Leesa demonstrated and gave Charlotte another piece. 'Throw it,' she urged, and threw another piece herself.

Charlotte watched as a brown and ginger duck waddled over to where the bread had landed and quickly ate it up. Charlotte looked down at her piece of bread and then quickly shoved it in her own mouth.

'No, Charlotte.' Leesa laughed and this time was too late to rescue the bread. 'I guess it's all right,' she conceded. It wasn't stale or mouldy so it wouldn't do any harm. 'You're a funny goose,' she told her niece, and a duck quacked loudly in protest. 'Ah, funny duck,' she corrected quickly.

It was almost forty-five minutes later that Leesa and Charlotte returned to the hospital. Just outside the ward was an area where patients could sit in the sunshine and enjoy the fresh air, even though most of them polluted it with cigarette smoke.

'Hey, Doc!' a masculine voice said as they walked past, and Leesa looked to see Jonno, lying on his bed, a cigarette in his hand. The entire bed, including the frame supporting the traction, had been wheeled out, which was common for bedridden patients.

There was a man sitting on a bench next to the bed. He was more heavily tattooed and had longer hair than his invalid friend.

'Hi.' She smiled at them and shifted Charlotte to her other hip.

'This your kid?' Jonno asked.

'No. Charlotte is my niece.'

'Yeah.' he nodded slowly. 'Everyone was talking about that accident your brother was in.'

'Brother-in-law,' she clarified. 'And his wife is my sister. They're both stabilising nicely.'

'This is my mate, Benno. Yeah, just up in Newcastle for a few days.'

'Yeah,' agreed Benno.

They chatted for a few minutes and Leesa discovered that both men had known each other since high school and had dropped out together to join a gang.

'I don't mean to sound critical—because I'm not,' Leesa added quickly, 'but why?'

'Neither of us had anyone to care about us. Our dads had nicked off when we were just kids and our mums had better things to do. The gang—they cared about us,' Jonno explained.

'So that's what you've been doing during the last ten years—just hanging out with the gang.'

'Yeah.' Jonno frowned. 'This accident's got me thinkin'. So many of me mates are either dead or worse than me. Benno here feels awful that he couldn't make it to the big ride. He was one of the lucky ones but he doesn't think so.'

Leesa looked at Benno who was concentrating on his cigarette.

'So what have you been thinking, Jonno?' Leesa asked the question softly. She was here to listen but only if they wanted to talk.

'I could've died. I *really* could've died. From now on, I wanna try and do things for me.' He looked straight up at the sky and mumbled, 'I wanna make my life better. There's got to be more to this life than riding my Harley all the time.'

Leesa looked across at Benno who was hiding behind his long hair. She thought she'd seen him nod slowly at Jonno's words.

'Sayin' such things makes me…you know…' He stopped and took a drag of his cigarette. 'All that stuff about loyalty to the gang an' all. I mean, what about loyalty to me? I just feel I've gotta start doin' what's right for me. I don't wanna spend any more time in the slammer.'

'Yeah,' Benno agreed, but still didn't come out from behind his hair.

'Nearly dyin' an' all—I just think there's more to this life and I've gotta reach out and grab it.'

Leesa was silent for a moment. 'I can arrange for you to speak to a social worker.'

'Nah,' Jonno protested quickly. 'I've had enough of them to last me a lifetime. Do no good, anyway.'

'The social worker on the ward is really very good—'

'Nah,' he repeated.

Charlotte was beginning to squirm in her arms and Leesa

transferred her to the opposite hip. 'How about the chaplain?'

'What—like a priest or somethin'?'

'Sort of. He's not a priest but the ward does have a chaplain assigned to it.'

Jonno thought it over, before saying slowly, 'Yeah. Yeah, all right. I'll speak to this chaplain and see what he says.'

'It's a start,' Leesa said with a smile. She looked across at Benno. 'I'm sure the chaplain would be happy for you to go with Jonno. If you wanted to,' she added so Benno didn't feel any pressure. 'I'll tell you one thing about starting a new life—only *you* can do it. If you're determined, then *nothing* should stand in your way.'

'Yeah,' both men replied in unison.

Charlotte began to whinge and rub her eyes. 'I'd better get her inside to her mother.'

Janet was sitting up, finishing a cup of tea. Angus was still on 'nil by mouth' and was looking slightly worse than when she'd left. Hamish was sitting by his bed.

Leesa moved Janet's table and cup out of the way and deposited Charlotte on the bed. The child snuggled against her mother and was content to stay there.

'It's time for her morning sleep,' Janet said. 'Did you bring a bottle?'

'I most certainly did. I'll make it up for you and hopefully the two of you can have a rest.' Leesa organised the bottle and soon Charlotte's eyes were drooping as she finished off the formula.

'So, tell us how this morning went. Did Charlotte wake during the evening?'

'Evening? You mean morning.' Leesa smiled and nodded. 'I took her into bed with me early this morning and we snuggled and slept, which was wonderful.' She couldn't look at Hamish while she spoke, remembering all too well the look of smouldering desire he'd appraised her with at the time.

'But wait until you hear what Uncle Hamish accomplished this morning.'

'Do you have to, Leesa?' Hamish cringed.

'He changed Charlotte's dirty nappy,' Leesa continued, ignoring his protest.

'Really?' Angus looked at his brother with surprise.

'Well done,' Janet praised. 'I knew you could do it.'

'It's not a pretty sight.' Angus shook his head, a smile lighting his features.

'You're telling me.' Hamish rolled his eyes.

'Poor Uncle Hamish did very well, considering I threw him in at the deep end. Charlotte was wonderful, waving her arms and legs everywhere and generally wriggling non-stop while the change was in process.'

'The usual.' Janet laughed and Angus joined in. Hamish simply scowled at the three of them but there was a twinkling light in his eyes.

'Just keep your voices down. If the rest of the staff find out about this, my reputation will be ruined.'

'On the contrary, Hamish. Your staff might actually begin to see you as a human being, rather than a force to be reckoned with,' Leesa pointed out, as they all enjoyed the moment.

'To think, my big brother is actually human enough to change a dirty nappy.' Angus laughed some more then cried out in agony.

Everyone was instantly silent, Hamish and Leesa on their feet and at his side. Leesa put a hand to his forehead.

'He's burning up. Why didn't you say something?' she scolded him, and buzzed for the nurse. Angus groaned again.

'Where's the pain?' Hamish asked.

'Abdo.' Angus gritted his teeth while Hamish probed his abdomen.

The nurse came rushing in. 'Order a blood test for full white cell count, stat,' Hamish ordered. 'Call Dr Dawson and have him here immediately.' The nurse left.

'What's wrong?' Janet asked, her voice laced with concern.

'Could be anything,' Hamish answered. 'With the car accident all sorts of scenarios are possible.'

Angus groaned again.

'What if it's not the accident?' Leesa asked. 'Janet, before the accident, can you think of anything that was wrong?'

'He had a bit of food poisoning a while ago but that's it.'

The nurse came back in. 'Dr Dawson is on his way in.'

'How's the pain?' Leesa asked.

'Still there but not as intense.'

The nurse took blood from Angus's good arm.

When she was finished, Leesa said, 'Here. I'll take that to Pathology and get a rush analysis done.'

'Good,' Hamish replied. 'My guess for the moment is appendicitis,' he told his brother. 'But let's see what the tests say. See if you can lean over their shoulders, Leesa. That way it might get done quicker.'

'Or they might kick me out,' she reasoned, but left regardless. Thankfully, the pathologists were willing to cooperate and performed the test immediately.

'White blood cell count elevated. Diagnosis of appendicitis confirmed,' the pathologist told her. She called the findings through to the ward.

Angus had been wheeled off to Theatre by the time she returned to the ward. She sat beside Janet's bed. Charlotte had snuggled down next to her mother and was sound asleep, completely missing the drama.

Janet looked at her sister with tears in her eyes.

'He'll be fine,' Leesa responded to the unspoken question. 'Hamish is with him and he'll be just fine. As hard as it might be, Janet, try and get some rest.'

'You'll stay?'

'I'll stay.'

CHAPTER SIX

FINALLY Janet started to doze and Leesa paced the room, waiting for some word from Hamish. She'd already heard from the nurses that he'd kicked up another stink when Carl Dawson had refused to allow him into Theatre to watch the operation.

Leesa rolled her eyes, knowing that Hamish had had to try. 'Typical,' she mumbled to herself. His protective instinct towards his family was both honourable and admirable and had been one of the qualities that had captivated her as a teenager.

Why wasn't she getting any news? How long did an appendectomy take? She looked at her watch for the thousandth time. 'I can't take it any more,' she said out loud, and, after checking her sleeping sister and niece, Leesa quickly went to the nurses' station.

'Have you heard anything?'

'No.'

'Mind if I use your phone?'

'Help yourself, but Mr Dawson doesn't like interruptions in his theatre.'

'Who does?' Leesa asked rhetorically. She called Theatre Sister and asked her to put her through to wherever Hamish was waiting. Leesa tapped her fingers on the counter impatiently while she waited.

'Mr O'Donnell,' Hamish barked down the phone.

'Where are you?'

'In the doctors' tearoom. I was just about to call you. How's Janet?'

'Sleeping for the moment. What's the news?'

'I've just called through to Theatre for the third time and

97

Carl informed me via the nurse that the appendix has been successfully removed..

'Thank goodness.' Leesa sighed.

'He should be out and in Recovery soon.'

'Good. I'd better get back to Janet. I promised her I wouldn't leave but didn't want to use the phone in the room in case I woke her.'

They rang off and Leesa returned to her sister's side. Both mother and daughter were still sleeping. Leesa slumped down in the chair, knowing that when Janet woke at least she'd have some good news to pass on.

Five minutes later Charlotte began to stir, and Leesa quickly picked her up. 'Shh.' She rocked her niece from side to side but Charlotte wouldn't listen. She started to cry, obviously not too impressed at waking up in a strange place. Leesa was just about to take her out of the room when Janet spoke.

'She's a terror some days, isn't she? Come here, darling.'

Leesa handed a very willing Charlotte back to her mother. Once there, she stopped crying and cuddled in again. Leesa felt a pang of envy for the comfort only a mother could have given. One day it would be here. One day…

'What's the news?'

Leesa schooled her thoughts. 'He should be coming out of Theatre now with no complications. One appendix successfully removed without perforation.'

Janet sighed with relief. 'I'm glad that's over.'

'You and me both. Now, is there anything I can get you? Feeling any pain?'

'No. Just having you here with me is helping a lot.'

'That's what sisters are for.'

'So how did things go last night with Hamish? I didn't realise he was staying at the house, too.'

'Angus asked him and, well, you know Hamish.'

'Yes, I do. Mr Protective. Maybe if you're living with

him, he'll begin to see you as the woman you really are. This could be your big break.'

Leesa smiled. Although she didn't want to lie to Janet, she also didn't want to reveal exactly what had happened with Hamish—especially during the past twenty-four hours. Up until now Leesa had always been open with Janet about her feelings for Hamish, but now that progress was being made, well, she didn't feel all that ready to share.

'You might be right. Do you think purposefully strutting around in skimpy nighties might do the trick?' Leesa's eyes twinkled with mischief.

Janet smiled. 'You want to get his attention, Leesa, not give him a heart attack.'

'No need to worry about that. I'm sure Hamish's heart is as strong as an ox's.'

'Yes, but you've been waiting for this for such a long time I'm just not sure he can cope with the full impact.'

'Then I'll have to take it agonisingly…slowly.' She whispered the last word, her thoughts immediately jumping to the incredible kiss they'd shared yesterday.

'He's not going to know what hit him,' Janet said, her face alight with happiness.

'It's good to see you smile,' Leesa said as Charlotte started to squirm.

'Any fruit in her bag?' Janet asked. 'She usually gets a bit hungry after her sleep.'

'Sure.' Leesa extracted a banana from the bag and peeled it for Charlotte. 'Actually, now might be a good time to tell me as much as you can about her routine. The more I can stick to it the better.'

Leesa stayed with Janet and Charlotte for the next few hours while they waited for Angus to be brought back to the ward. She played games with Charlotte and they watched a bit of television while Janet snoozed.

Finally, both brothers returned to the ward, Angus still rather drowsy but pleased to be back near his family.

At half past four Hamish ordered everyone to say their goodbyes so they could take Charlotte home and start her evening routine. 'I promised Gabby we'd be back by then,' he volunteered.

Charlotte was, naturally, not too happy at being separated from both her parents but stopped crying once she was strapped securely in her car seat.

'Janet's told me all about Charlotte's usual routine so between the three of us hopefully we'll be able to stick to it.'

'Wouldn't Gabby know about her routine?' he asked.

'She's only been looking after Charlotte for the past week and a half, and only on sporadic days. Not at night. Angus's and Janet's trip to Moss Vale yesterday, to attend that seminar, was a once-off. Not that I don't have every faith in Gabby—I do. It's just so important for a child to stay in its routine—especially when there's such an enormous disruption to her daily life.'

'Well she has a very devoted aunty,' Hamish replied with a smile.

'And uncle. I saw you crawling around with her outside. You pretend to be keeping your distance. We all know you love her and you'll hold her when asked, but today was the first day you've really *connected* with her...isn't it?' Leesa asked the probing question quietly. She knew the observation would probably bother Hamish, not because she'd witnessed it but because she understood him.

'Yes,' he answered after a moment. 'What gave me away? Feeding her breakfast or the nappy change?'

Leesa laughed. 'Definitely the nappy change. Would you like to try bathing her tonight?'

He nodded. 'I'm feeling game. Why not?'

When they arrived home Gabby was sitting at the kitchen table with books scattered everywhere.

'I needed to get some study done so I've been here for a few hours. My home is like a three-ringed circus.'

'Glad you were able to take advantage of the peace and quiet,' Leesa answered as she released Charlotte onto the floor. The baby crawled over to Gabby then pulled herself up, using the chair legs as guidance. Gabby reached down and picked her up for a quick cuddle before Charlotte was squirming to get back to the floor.

'So, boss,' Hamish said, and turned to Leesa. 'What's the first item of Charlotte's routine we need to take care of?'

Gabby packed up her books and between the three of them they organised dinner and sat down to eat as a 'family'.

'That was delicious, Gabby. Thank you,' Hamish said as he finished his meal of shepherd's pie with vegetables. 'Just as well you have some cooking skills or we may have been left to the mercy of Leesa's!'

'I'm not the only one who can't cook, Hamish. You're not much better, and why should the cooking always be left to the women? Most chefs in the big chain hotels are men.'

'Simmer down.' Hamish laughed and Gabby joined in, realising they were teasing each other. 'She just loves getting on her soap box,' he told Gabby in a stage whisper.

'I'll clear up,' Leesa said as she collected the plates and glasses. 'Hamish, would you mind running the bath?'

'Oh, I'll do that,' Gabby said as she stood.

'No.' Leesa said. 'Hamish *wants* to do it.'

'OK,' Gabby said slowly, looking from one to the other. When Hamish left the room, Gabby asked, 'He doesn't have a clue what he's in for, does he?'

'Nope.' Leesa smiled sweetly. 'And that's the whole idea.'

'Whew!' Hamish said a few hours later when Charlotte was finally asleep. 'I didn't think she'd ever stop. Where does she get her energy from?'

Leesa laughed. 'She's just a normal, healthy child. Just wait until she's running around.'

He sat down on the lounge. 'It gets worse?' he asked as he ran his fingers through his still damp hair.

'I've often heard Janet say, "It doesn't get worse, it just gets different."'

'Lucky Janet and Angus, then.' Hamish accepted the cup of tea she offered him. 'Where's Gabby?'

'Doing some more studying. She has a test on Monday, but only for a few hours, so I've arranged for Charlotte to go to Karen—Janet's and Angus's secretary/receptionist.'

'Good thinking.'

'Karen said the clinic is fairly quiet for the week and the locum can handle what comes in. Besides, Charlotte knows Karen very well so it works out terrifically.'

'Do you realise,' he asked in quiet amazement when she joined him, 'that by the time Charlotte had finished in the bath, there was more water *outside* the bath than in? One little splash from her cute, chubby hand and there was Uncle Hamish completely drenched.'

Leesa laughed again. She and Gabby had been hard-pressed to contain their laughter when Hamish had appeared with a clean little girl wrapped in a big fluffy towel while he'd been completely saturated.

'She does it to everyone the first time they bathe her,' Leesa explained. 'I think it's her way of initiating people.'

'So she's drenched you?'

'Oh, yes, but now I know the secret.'

'Do tell.'

'Distract her from splashing with other toys. If that doesn't work, Janet will quickly wash her and, *voilà*, the bath is over. Children are by no means stupid. They know who they can push around and who they can't.'

'Great! My eleven-month-old niece is pushing her uncle around.'

'What can I say—she's a woman! It's in the genes.'

'You're thoroughly enjoying this, aren't you?'

'By *this* do you mean your initiation into humanity?'

Hamish's smile slowly disappeared and he turned to face Leesa. 'I'm just beginning to realise that *this,* as you call it, is a conspiracy. Made up not only of you and my niece but my brother and sister-in-law as well.' His words weren't affronted, merely stating a fact.

'Keep going,' she encouraged, not refuting a word he said. 'Both sets of parents are also in this conspiracy.'

'Great!' He threw his hands in the air and gave her a small smile. 'Not only is my niece pushing me around, but the rest of my family—and extended family—are ganging up on me to make me…more human.'

'Do you mind?'

'Do I have the option?'

'Not really.' Leesa shrugged matter-of-factly. She watched as he drained his cup and set it on the coffee-table. She did the same, before saying, 'Seriously, Hamish, you were getting to the stage where you weren't showing *any* emotion at all. Not in Theatre, not in clinics, not in meetings, not in family situations. You were just so…neutral.'

'Maybe I like neutral.' Did she hear a slightly defensive tone in his words?

'Neutral isn't healthy.' She reached out and took his hand in hers. 'I don't profess to know much about your marriage but your parents accredit your emotional withdrawal from life to that.'

'Do you have round-table discussions about me?' he enquired.

'It's not like that,' Leesa said quickly.

'I know. I also know the motive for this conspiracy is love. If it weren't, I guess I would be more offended than I am.' He raised her hand to his lips. 'I know my mother's been praising your virtues for quite a few years—that the entire family think we're a perfect match—but believe me when I say I'm not so sure.'

Leesa felt tears begin to prick behind her eyes. 'You think I deserve better than you.'

'Yes.' He leaned forward and placed his other hand at the back of her neck, drawing her to him for a kiss. When their lips met it was as though Leesa were coming home, and she knew he was wrong.

She applied her words of inspiration for Jonno to herself. If *she* wanted to change her life, then *she* was the only one who could do it. If she *really* wanted Hamish—and she did—then she was positive he would one day be her husband. *Regardless* of what he said.

'Yet at the moment,' he whispered, their lips only millimetres apart, 'I can't seem to control myself when I'm around you. I don't want you to be hurt when things don't work out. I want to protect you from that, but at the same time I want all you'll give me—and I know that will be everything you have.'

'Just kiss me,' she replied, and brought her lips back into contact with his.

This kiss was more of what she had expected yesterday. Their lips were both starved from lack of contact and the playful assault Hamish started with soon turned into a heated onslaught of all emotions.

Leesa moved in closer and thrust her fingers into his damp hair, enjoying the sensation of messing it up while ensuring he didn't withdraw from their embrace. His tongue was hot and probing in her mouth and she welcomed it eagerly.

When he eventually drew back it was to plant small kisses down her neck and around the neckline of her T-shirt. Leesa threw back her head and breathed in deeply through her mouth.

'Hamish,' she whispered as his kisses moved back up her neck, causing a delicious wave of desire to wash over her. She looked at him through half-closed lashes, the sound of her pounding heart reverberating in her ears. 'I'm on fire.'

'You're not the only one,' he replied, and pressed his lips firmly to her own again.

The noise that filled the room startled them both, and they instantly froze before realising it was Charlotte, stirring. They both looked at the baby monitor that sat on the table.

Leesa took a deep, steadying breath. 'Perhaps I should go to her.' As soon as the words were out of her mouth they heard Gabby go into the room, offering comfort.

'I guess not,' Hamish said, but released his hold on Leesa. He stood and raked a hand through his very rumpled hair. 'I forgot where I was for a moment. You,' he went on, 'have a habit of making me do that.'

Leesa smiled, pleased with the backhanded compliment.

'No, don't smile,' he groaned with frustration. He looked at his watch. 'It's only half past eight. We have a teenager and a baby in the house as chaperones but, more importantly, we need to take…whatever it is between us a little more slowly.'

'My sentiments exactly,' Leesa agreed. Rushing Hamish would serve no purpose and this was one conspiracy that *had* to be successful.

They sat down—close to each other—and watched a movie. Gabby came down for a snack and declined to watch the movie with them, knowing she should be studying.

'Admirable quality,' Hamish responded when she left.

The easy camaraderie they shared returned, and they enjoyed the mystery movie they were watching. When it finished they both checked on Charlotte, who was sound asleep, before Hamish kissed Leesa—briefly—goodnight and went to his own room. She heard the door shut firmly behind him.

'Everything is moving along perfectly,' she told her reflection as she brushed her hair. 'Soon Hamish and I will be as happy as our siblings. Once more the O'Donnell and Stevenson families will be united through holy matrimony.'

Sunday turned out to be similar to Saturday, with Hamish and Leesa spending a good deal of their time at the hospital with Janet and Angus. Little Charlotte loved being with her parents, but when it came to separation time another tantrum occurred. Not that anyone blamed her, but it did make it harder for Janet and Angus to watch their daughter leave.

'Knowing that you and Hamish are there with her makes all the difference in the world,' Janet told Leesa as they kissed goodbye.

Monday morning dawned bright and early, with Charlotte once again crying her way into Aunty Leesa's bed in the early hours of the morning.

'Perhaps we shouldn't encourage it?' Hamish suggested as they ate breakfast. Gabby had crammed a piece of toast in her mouth and headed off to the university library to do more studying.

'It's only for a short time and, besides, the poor little darling has had her life turned upside down. What's a bit of extra cuddling here and there?'

'I suppose. Although once Janet and Angus come home, they'll have a hard time getting her back into her proper sleeping routine,' he pointed out.

'By which time she'll probably have both sets of grandparents here to do her bidding, and they'll all be taking turns fighting over who wakes up at three a.m. to give Charlotte a cuddle!'

Hamish turned his attention back to Charlotte and spooned another mouthful of cereal in.

'That's it, isn't it?' Leesa looked at him with a smile. 'That's what you're really miffed about. The fact that three nights in a row Charlotte has come into bed with me.' Leesa finished eating and stood to take her bowl to the dishwasher. She stopped and bent down to whisper in Hamish's ear, 'So who do you want to cuddle more? Charlotte? Or me?'

His answer was a grunt of derision that made Leesa's smile even bigger.

'I thought so,' she said as she continued on her way. 'You want us both. Typical male!'

At this statement Charlotte gurgled something and clapped her hands.

'Yes, darling. I'd half expected you to be on his side. I'll finish getting ready then pack your baby-bag.'

'We may as well take one car,' Hamish said as she was walking out of the room. She stopped and turned to face him. 'It makes sense.' He shrugged and forced another mouthful into Charlotte.

'Perfect sense,' Leesa told him, and continued on her way.

They dropped Charlotte off at the general practice that Janet and Angus owned. Karen was only too happy to see Charlotte, and by the way the child almost launched herself at the secretary/receptionist the feeling was obviously mutual.

After parking in the doctors' car park, they walked to the theatre block.

'I'll get changed, before going down to the ward to see how Jonno's doing and to check on Janet's and Angus's progress,' Leesa told Hamish outside the male and female changing rooms.

'Good. I'll meet you back here in a few minutes and we can go down together. We'll do a quick ward round while Jonno's being prepped for Theatre and then get this pelvic fracture out of the way.'

'OK,' she replied, and pushed open the changing room door. It's working, it's working, she thought excitedly. He's wanting to do everything *with* me rather than separately.

Leesa made sure she didn't keep him waiting and they

headed off to the ward. Caroline Metcalfe stopped them both as they were about to leave Theatres.

'And just where do you think you're both sneaking off to?' she asked. 'Your list starts in half an hour, Mr O'Donnell.'

'I know,' he replied as they both turned around to face her. 'We'll be back.'

'They're both looking a lot better this morning,' Caroline volunteered.

'How do—?' Leesa asked when Caroline interrupted her.

'I doubt if there's a member of your staff who hasn't kept a close eye or checked up on your family members. Not for gossip's sake but because they're genuinely concerned.'

'Thanks for the update.' Leesa smiled. 'But we'd still like to quickly say good morning.'

'Of course you do. I'll stall if I have to.'

'Leesa,' Hamish barked as he walked off down the corridor.

'Thanks, Caroline,' Leesa acknowledged, and quickly caught up to Hamish.

'There's no need for rudeness,' she told him as she took the stairs down two levels to the orthopaedic wards.

'Why waste precious time, standing around talking? We now only have half an hour.'

'Yes, boss.' She gave him a mock salute.

'I hope you're going to lose this silly attitude by the time we get to Theatre. I need your complete concentration for Jonno's pelvic fracture operation.'

'Yes, boss,' she reiterated happily. She just couldn't help it. At this single moment in time she was happy. Very happy. And the man beside her was the cause of that happiness.

They had just checked Jonno when Pete, the anaesthetist, arrived so they left their patient in his capable hands. After doing a quick ward round, they were left with just under five minutes to see their siblings.

Caroline had, indeed, spoken truthfully. Janet was sitting up, eating a light breakfast, when they walked in and Angus was sipping a cup of tea.

'Twenty-four hours can make a lot of difference,' he pointed out when they both remarked on how well he looked. 'As well as having my lovely wife beside me.'

They stayed for a few more minutes before Hamish insisted they leave and return to Theatre.

'I'll try and catch up after Theatre and before clinic,' Leesa promised as Hamish all but dragged her from the room.

Jonno's pelvic fracture was the only scheduled operation on the list that morning but they required the full four hours to get through it.

He had a fracture to the right acetabulum and symphysis pubis which Hamish fixed, using open reduction and internal fixation. Because the acetabulum was the socket into which the spherical head of the femur fitted, Hamish had to use several different approaches to ensure it was securely and accurately fixed with plates and screws.

'Check X-ray, please,' he stated blandly as the radiographer wheeled the portable X-ray equipment over to do his bidding.

When the films were developed and Hamish was satisfied, they turned their attention to the symphysis pubis.

'This is an easier bone to get to, ladies and gentleman,' Hamish told the theatre staff, 'so, although it appears we're running behind time at the moment, we shouldn't be too much longer. Rest assured, you should all get at least twenty whole minutes for a lunch-break.'

'What luxury,' Pete replied with forced joviality.

Hamish was true to his word and soon he started closing the wound in layers, stapling the skin closed.

As they de-gowned, Hamish said, 'Now you can go and

spend a bit more time with your sister. I know how you girls like to talk.'

'Angus will be in the room as well. Won't you join us?'

'Sorry. I have a lunchtime meeting to attend. I'll see you in clinic.'

The rest of the theatre staff were busy cleaning up and doing further instrument counts. They were alone and Leesa quickly leaned over and kissed him on the lips.

'What was that for?' he asked with surprise, checking over his shoulder that no one had seen it.

'For making sure I had time to spend with my sister. I know you're not the type of person to rush your operations, but you were making every effort to ensure we finished on time. Thank you.'

His gaze held hers and he smiled. 'You're welcome.' He returned the brief kiss, before walking out the door.

'Ahem,' a female voice said from behind her, and Leesa quickly spun around to see Caroline coming through the door from Theatre. 'I don't want you to think I was eavesdropping because I wasn't. I'd also like you to know that I'm the soul of discretion and what I just witnessed will never be repeated to anyone, but I must say it's about time Mr O'Donnell saw you in your true light. Little sister, indeed!'

Leesa smiled. 'Let's hope no one else finds out. Not that it would bother me, but Hamish would hit the ceiling if our *new* relationship was leaked to the hospital grapevine.'

'He's a very private man,' Caroline stated. 'As I've only known you for the past month, I guess I have a more objective view than other staff who've been here for years. Everyone sees you as family—brother and sister—so even if they'd witnessed the kiss *you* gave him, they probably wouldn't have thought anything of it. It was *him* kissing you that spoke volumes.'

'I guess we'll have to be a bit more careful.'

Caroline smiled. 'Go and see your sister.'

*   *   *

Throughout the next week Leesa and Hamish fell into an easy routine. They would leave the house every morning after spending a bit of time with Charlotte, before leaving her in Gabby's capable hands, driving to the hospital in Hamish's car and spending a few quick minutes with their siblings before they started their day.

Janet and Angus had both progressed nicely and were busy with physiotherapists and rehabilitation counsellors, getting back into the swing of things. Gabby brought Charlotte to the hospital every afternoon to spend time with her parents before they all returned home for dinner.

Both Hamish and Leesa would bring their paperwork home and sit at the large dining table after Charlotte had gone to bed and work in a companionable silence, breaking it every now and then to check a detail or offer a drink.

Their kisses became more intense but beyond that Hamish would kiss her goodnight at her door before leaving her. If Gabby knew of their closer relationship, she kept it to herself.

Mr Lewis's weight-bearing was still advancing slowly but steadily.

'I've spent quite a bit of time with your sister and her husband lately,' he commented to Leesa on Friday morning. After the ward round, she'd returned to his bedside for a chat.

'Yes, Janet told me.'

'Lovely couple,' he remarked. 'It's been good to sit out in the sun and have a chat. Their little Charlotte is a darling and the young nanny they've employed is quite taken with her—but, then, you'd already know that,' he finished.

'Gabby's very loving yet firm with Charlotte.'

'It's rare to see those qualities in someone of her age. She has her head on straight.'

'It's a relief to know Charlotte is happy in Gabby's company. It's been hard on Charlotte, not having her parents around, so we've all tried to create the next best thing.'

'You and Mr O'Donnell are to be commended. That's another thing you don't see a lot of nowadays—families sticking together. I hardly see my own children. Too busy with their own lives.' He looked sadly down at his hands. 'I guess that's why I've enjoyed chatting with your sister and brother-in-law.' He raised his head and looked at Leesa with tears in his eyes. 'A fine pair.'

'They've also enjoyed your chats.' Leesa leaned over and kissed Mr Lewis on the cheek. 'You know, over the years I've met quite a few patients who I just seem to…click with. Those same people are still very close friends.' She reached out for Mr Lewis's hand and squeezed it. 'I know things are difficult for you now and soon you'll be transferred to the rehabilitation hospital for a few weeks, but promise me…' She looked him in the eyes. 'Promise me you'll keep in touch. Not only with myself and Mr O'Donnell but our family as well.'

The smile that lit Mr Lewis's face wavered slightly, a tear dropping from his eye onto his withered old cheek. Not trusting himself to speak, he merely nodded.

'Good. I'll hold you to it.' Leesa's pager beeped. She checked the number—Radiology. After giving his hand another quick squeeze, she left his bedside to answer it.

Radiology informed her that the X-rays of Jonno's pelvis were now ready for her to collect. Leesa picked them up and went straight to Hamish's office. As they viewed them, Hamish was very pleased with the results one week post-op. His arm came around her waist and he leaned closer.

'You smell incredible,' he whispered. 'Are you trying to drive me insane on purpose?' He placed a soft kiss on her lips.

'Hamish, I've been trying to drive you insane for years.'

'It's been working.' With superb control he took a step away and raked his fingers through his hair. 'More now than ever before.'

'Good.' She smiled.

Later that morning, Leesa sneaked down to spend some time with Janet. They sat outside in the sunshine, talking quietly.

'At least you've accomplished your goal,' Janet said. 'Hamish now sees you for the desirable woman you are. You seem happier than I can remember. Have either of you mentioned your new relationship to the parents?'

'I haven't and I'm almost certain Hamish hasn't. As far as I know, he hasn't even said anything to Angus.'

'Hamish isn't your kiss-and-tell type. Neither was Angus, if you remember. What that man put me through!' Janet reflected for a moment, before smiling. 'It's simply the way Hamish is around you now that shows us how he feels. He'll touch your arm or hold your fingers for just a fraction of a second longer than he would if the touch were brotherly. His gaze will linger on you when you walk in or out of the room.' Janet laughed. 'It's such a relief to see him appreciate you for who you are after all these years.'

'It's also shown me a side of him I knew existed but never experienced.' Leesa's eyes were glazed in wonderment.

'Hamish has a heart as big as the Kimberlies and it's so nice to see him opening it up to someone who truly loves him.'

'Speaking of which…' Leesa checked her watch '…we have a research meeting to go to before clinic this afternoon, so I'd better get to his office.' She stood. 'Do you want to stay out here or come back inside? I know you turned down the offer of a wheelchair as you preferred to walk, which is good because that's what the physio has ordered, but I can always go and get you a wheelchair.'

'I'm fine.' Janet accepted a hug from her sister. 'You go. I'll be fine. Angus should be finished with his physio soon and will probably join me. The sunshine is too good to miss.'

Leesa hurried to Hamish's office, knocking briefly before

she entered. He was standing beside his desk, leafing through a thick file, and looked up.

'I was just about to page you but guessed you were having a chat with Janet before Charlotte and Gabby arrived.'

'Yes. Angus was at physio so it was nice to have her to myself.'

He nodded his understanding. 'If you're ready…' He put the file down. 'We'll get going but only after you give me a kiss.' He held out his arms to her and she went straight to him. 'I haven't had one since we left home this morning and I'm starting to have withdrawal symptoms.'

'I thought you'd never ask.'

Hamish bent his head and found her lips with practised ease. Leesa closed her eyes, enjoying the sensation of being pressed against his firm chest. His tongue probed and she opened her mouth in acceptance.

There was a brisk knock at the door before it opened.

Leesa sprang from his arms at the same instant he pushed her away.

'Sorry,' Nanette, one of the junior secretaries, quickly apologised, although the gleam that lit her face clearly displayed that she wasn't sorry at all. 'You need this file for your meeting later this afternoon. I just thought I'd bring it in.'

'Thanks,' Hamish replied, and took the file from her.

The secretary quickly left but not before glancing over her shoulder once more, making no attempt to hide her increasing smile.

'Great!' Hamish slammed the file onto his desk. His tone was cold and distant. 'She's the biggest gossip in the department. It will be all through the hospital grapevine within the next hour.'

'Hamish, it was bound to happen.'

'No, Leesa. We should have been more careful. As head of the department, it's vital that I maintain a certain standard—a certain distance.'

'Well, I'm sure you're also allowed to show that you're human.'

'Human! Something you and the rest of our families have conspired to prove.'

'Hamish, you're blowing this way out of proportion,' Leesa tried to soothe, and reached out a hand to him.

He moved away from her. 'Not here, Leesa. Not within a ten-mile radius of the hospital. You know I care for you deeply and now that this…this piece of gossip will be spread about the hospital, our every action will be an open discussion for anyone and everyone.'

'Withdrawing completely may only add fuel to the fire.'

'Perhaps, but that's the way it's going to be.' He looked at his watch. 'Now we're late!' He strode angrily out his office, his head down, not meeting anyone's gaze. Leesa followed but didn't even attempt to catch up to him.

His secretary gave her a wide *knowing* smile and Leesa simply smiled back. The afternoon was going to drag on and they still had to get through their outpatient clinic.

CHAPTER SEVEN

BEFORE they left the hospital that Friday night, Hamish had reinstated both of them back onto the emergency call roster. This meant that once a week each of them would take a turn being responsible for any emergencies that came into Casualty.

Before Janet's and Angus's accident, Leesa had always accompanied Hamish for the on-call shifts but now he had rostered her on by herself.

'After all,' he reasoned, 'you are a qualified orthopaedic surgeon.' They were driving home from the hospital in his car and this was their first exchange of words since he'd stormed out of his office, apart from the few monosyllables she'd managed to pry from him during the afternoon.

She looked at the copy of the roster he'd handed her. He was down for tomorrow and she was down for Sunday. 'That should make for a fun weekend,' she murmured dryly. Hamish didn't reply and she sighed. 'We should talk about what happened, Hamish. How is this going to affect us?'

'As far as I'm concerned, Leesa, away from the hospital we can pursue a…relationship, if that's what you want, but as soon as we enter the hospital gates we treat each other as colleagues.'

'If that's what *I* want?' she said, a note of disbelief in her tone. 'What about *you*, Hamish? Do *you* want to pursue a relationship?'

'Leesa, that's not what I meant.'

'That's what you said, Hamish. Are you attracted to me?'

'Yes,' he said after a moment's hesitation.

116

'Do you want to stop spending more quality time with me?'

'No.'

The fact that he'd answered that question more quickly gave Leesa a small vestige of hope.

'Good. Then how about we take Charlotte to the park tomorrow before we go to the hospital?'

'I have no objection to that, except we don't choose a park close to the hospital.'

'Hamish, whether you like it or not, we're connected by family so even at the hospital you'll still need to acknowledge that you at least *know* me.'

'You're over-exaggerating as usual.'

Leesa sighed. 'I'm not over-exaggerating, Hamish. I was being...sarcastic.'

'Sarcasm doesn't suit you.' He pulled into Janet's and Angus's driveway and switched off the engine. 'Look.' He reached for her hand and held it in his, his tone calm. 'I still want to be with you, but when I'm in or near the hospital I just think we should keep our distance. I lost count of how many curious glances I received from all the staff in Outpatients—both clerical and medical.'

'I know. I was there, too, remember. You're not the only one the hospital is talking about, but why does it bother you so much? Why shouldn't you have a relationship?'

'It's none of their business.' He dropped her hand and took the keys out of the ignition.

'I agree. I also agree we shouldn't...*flaunt* our relationship, for want of a better word, in the hospital but you're just taking things a bit too far.'

Leesa reached out a hand and smoothed his hair back from his forehead. 'I know this is hard for you, especially as you're the type of person to keep an emotional distance from people, but it's not the end of the world. We're going to be talked about whether we like it or not, whether we're openly amorous or not, whether we ignore each other or not.

'I *know* you,' she continued. 'I've known you for most of my life and I understand how you think.'

'Great,' he said with a nervous laugh. 'Another part of me that's no longer a secret.'

'Hamish, I don't really care what people say about us, but I want you to know that I respect your feelings and will abide by your decision to keep our ''hospital'' life strictly business. But that doesn't mean I'm going to stop caring about you. I want to be with you. I want to spend time with you.' Steady, Leesa, she told herself. Confessing too much at this time might scare him off for good.

'If we go out together on the weekend and someone from the hospital just happens to see us, I'm not going to pretend there's nothing going on between us. So from now on we'll maintain our distance around the hospital.'

'Thank you,' he said, and leaned forward, placing his palm against her cheek. 'It means a lot, Leesa.' He brought his lips to hers in a tired but happy kiss. 'Let's go inside and get some sleep. I've heard what you've said, but now that I've put us back onto the emergency roster I can't change it.'

'I understand.' She opened the car door, reaching for her briefcase as she went. They walked to the back door and Hamish unlocked it.

'Another thing. I suggest we take separate cars to the hospital from now on.'

'Sure,' Leesa agreed nonchalantly. 'It was fun while it lasted.'

'What's *that* supposed to mean?' he asked in a slightly defensive tone.

'Calm down. It only means my days of having my personal and, I might add, very attractive and sexy chauffeur are over.'

He smiled and her heart sang. 'Did I mention I was tired?' he said as he held the door open for her to enter.

'No. You never said anything about being tired. You mentioned the emergency roster and almost implied that we should get some sleep, but you never actually said that—'

'Enough! Let's have a cup of tea and an early night.'

'Yes, boss,' she replied meekly, but couldn't resist the opportunity to swish her hips as she walked into the house in front of him. At least she'd managed to talk calmly about their new predicament with Hamish and stop him from withdrawing. Getting him into a good mood had been a bonus!

I've still got it, she told herself as she changed for bed forty-five minutes later, still savouring the taste of Hamish's goodnight kiss on her lips.

Throughout the weekend, Leesa and Hamish were hard pressed to find time alone. Either they were at home with Gabby and Charlotte or at the hospital with Janet and Angus. Hamish was on call and then Leesa, so by the time they finished operating on Monday morning Leesa had all but given up hope of being alone with Hamish.

She decided to take matters into her own hands that afternoon and during clinic rang the extension of Hamish's consulting room.

'Mr O'Donnell,' he barked into the mouthpiece.

'Seven-thirty tonight at the Bogey Hole. Don't be late.'

'Thank you,' he said briskly, before hanging up.

Leesa smiled to herself as she mentally went through what she would need to prepare for a night of star-gazing with Hamish. She gave Gabby a quick call, catching the nanny as she and Charlotte were heading out the door on their way to the hospital for their daily visit.

'Hamish and I will be home late tonight.'

'Do you have a secret rendezvous planned?' Gabby asked, and Leesa could tell she was smiling.

'Yes.'

'Good. You both deserve some time away from everyone and everything—even if it's only for a few hours. Don't worry about Charlotte.'

'Thanks, Gabby. We won't be too late.'

'Not a problem. I'd better get going before Charlotte decides to get into more mischief.'

They rang off, Leesa feeling decidedly pleased with herself.

'Dr Stevenson?' The clinic nurse poked her head around the door, interrupting Leesa's thoughts. 'Ready for your next patient?'

'Yes,' Leesa replied with a smile, relieved that she'd taken measures into her own hands to ensure she and Hamish spent some time alone. 'Send…' Leesa checked her clinic list '…Mrs Leonard in.'

Mrs Leonard was wheeled in by an orderly.

'He said the chair would be more comfortable,' Mrs Leonard told Leesa with a shaky smile.

'He's probably right,' Leesa replied. 'I gather that knee isn't doing you any good.'

'No, dear. This morning it was so painful that I rang the clinic, hoping I could get an appointment. I know you're usually booked up for days, but when I told the girl on the phone that Mr O'Donnell had already operated on me she gave me an appointment straight away.'

'Good. Let me help you onto the examination couch and I'll take a look at your knee.'

Once Mrs Leonard was comfortable, Leesa began to go through her examination. 'Tell me exactly what happened this morning,' she said as she continued.

'My knee was sore when I woke up and it hurt to put my weight onto it. Richard…' A gleam twinkled in the older woman's eyes at the mention of her husband.

'Richard helped me to bathe, but when I was trying to get dressed it gave way. Just like that. One minute I was standing up and the next I was on the ground and in agony. Well, anyway, Richard gave me some of those tablets you prescribed for the pain after my last arthroscopy and that helped to dull things a bit, but we decided it was best to come in straight away and see you or Mr O'Donnell.'

'You did the right thing.' Leesa patted her patient's hand. 'The knee is back into position now, but I would guess that you dislocated it which caused you to fall. I would like you to have X-rays to check on the level of the rheumatoid arthritis in the joint but chances are, and we've discussed this before, you'll need a knee replacement on this side.'

Mrs Leonard nodded as Leesa helped her back into the wheelchair. She buzzed through to Reception and requested another orderly to take Mrs Leonard to Radiology.

'I guess it had to happen sooner or later,' Mrs Leonard sighed. 'I wonder if there will be anything left of me, thanks to the arthritis. Knee replacements, hip replacements, finger-joint replacements—I'm beginning to feel like the bionic woman.'

Leesa smiled. 'What's good to see is that you still have your sense of humour. Keep that, and you can't go wrong in life.'

The orderly entered and whisked Mrs Leonard down to Radiology. Leesa saw four more patients before Mrs Leonard was once again wheeled back into her consulting room—radiographs in tow.

'I'll need to admit you tonight, Mrs Leonard,' Leesa told her. 'I don't want to wait until Mr O'Donnell's operating list on Friday morning so I'll see if I can squeeze you in on the end of the emergency list tomorrow morning. First, though, I'd like Hamish to second the diagnosis.'

She dialled his extension and waited for his brisk reply before she said,

'Hamish, are you free?'

'For you, gorgeous, anything,' he said very softly into the phone, and Leesa smiled, turning her head away from Mrs Leonard.

'I'll take that as a yes. Do you have a few moments to spare for Mrs Leonard?'

'Knee dislocated?' he asked in his normal tone.

'Yes.'

'I'll be right there.'

Within seconds there was a knock at her door and Hamish entered, greeting Mrs Leonard. Leesa also noted that he left the door open—so none of the staff would think anything was going on in Leesa's consulting room other than the practice of medicine.

He took a quick look at the X-rays and agreed with Leesa's diagnosis.

'If Dr Stevenson can't get you tacked onto the end of emergency time tomorrow, I'm sure I'll be able to persuade one of my colleagues to allow us to perform your operation during their theatre time. Either way, you need that operation tomorrow.'

'Thank you,' Mrs Leonard said, reaching out a shaking hand to Hamish. 'And you, too, Dr Stevenson. Thank you.'

'I'll organise for a bed in the ward and have the orderly take you down. Is Mr Leonard with you?' Leesa asked.

'Yes. Richard's here. He's out in the waiting room.'

'He'll need to make arrangements for you to stay for a few nights.' Hamish took hold of the wheelchair handles. 'Let me take you out to him while Leesa organises that bed for you.'

With that, Hamish wheeled Mrs Leonard out, and that was the last Leesa saw of him until the end of the clinic. She was writing up the last of her patent notes when he knocked on her open door.

'Finished?' He didn't make any attempt to enter her consulting room but stayed in the corridor where everyone could see him.

'Yes.'

'We'll go to the ward to check on Mrs Leonard and see how Mr Lewis is progressing. His physiotherapist called to say his progress today was exemplary and, in her opinion, Mr Lewis can be transferred to the rehabilitation hospital any time we like.'

'OK.' Leesa scrawled her signature to the notes and placed them on the large pile of completed cases. 'Let's go.' She pushed her pen into the pocket of her white coat which hung open over her short black skirt and red knit top.

They said goodnight to the reception staff and were almost out of the door when they heard giggles of laughter. Hamish ground his teeth.

'Just let it go,' she told him as they walked towards the ward. 'The more you react, the more ammunition it gives them.'

'But it's all innocent. We're just going to the ward to check on some patients.'

'What the grapevine doesn't know, Hamish, is made up. The last I heard, I was supposedly pregnant.'

'What?' he exploded, and she quickly shushed him.

'Relax. They'll all find out in a few months time that it isn't true. We're just the flavour of the month. The more we react, the worse it will become. Just let it go. We have patients to see.'

Mrs Leonard was settled in a ward with three other women, but the nurse had drawn the curtains around her bed for a bit of privacy. Mr Leonard sat in a chair by the bed, holding his wife's hand.

'How are things going?' Leesa asked, and Mrs Leonard nodded.

'Just fine, dear.'

'I've made some calls,' Hamish told them, 'and arranged for your operation at nine-fifteen tomorrow morning.'

'Oh, dear.' Mrs Leonard looked worried. 'I hope no one else was inconvenienced because of me.'

'No. Our colleague, Jake Tindall, had a cancellation on his list so you get to take the spot.'

'That's very nice of him,' Mrs Leonard remarked. 'Please, thank him for me.'

'I will.' Hamish smiled.

'So you'll be fasting from just after teatime tonight,' Leesa explained, and went through the pre- and post-operative regimes with Mrs Leonard. 'Then afterwards you'll have extensive physio…' Leesa stopped and smiled at her patient. 'You know the drill. You've been through it all so many times before that *you* could probably tell me what will happen next.'

'True.' Mrs Leonard smiled. 'Physio, physio and more physio.'

'Correct.' Leesa's beeper sounded. She turned it off and quickly checked the number.

'You go and answer that, dear. We'll be fine, my Richard and I,' she said, clutching her husband's hand more tightly. 'We'll let you know if we have any questions.'

'All right. Try and sleep well and we'll see you tomorrow before the operation.'

They left the female end of the ward and went to the male end to check on Mr Lewis.

'I'll just answer this call,' Leesa told Hamish. 'I won't be long.' She ducked into the sister's office for a bit of privacy and rang the number on her beeper. It was the catering place who were preparing a wonderful goody basket for Leesa's special night out with Hamish.

'We close at five-thirty,' the woman told her. 'Is there anywhere we can deliver it to?'

'No.' Leesa checked her watch. It was almost five-thirty now. There was no way she would make it in time. She thought fast, before saying, 'Is it possible to have it delivered to the hospital?'

'Of course, dear. What ward?'

'Send it to Mr and Mrs Angus O'Donnell—room four, Orthopaedic ward two in the Grenfel Wing.' The shop assistant repeated the details and told Leesa the basket was on its way out of the door with the delivery boy as she spoke.

Leesa quickly replaced the receiver and raced to Janet's and Angus's room. She poked her head around the door and was about to say something when she realised there were two nurses in the room, chatting.

'I'll be back in a minute,' she told them, and hurried to review Mr Lewis with Hamish.

'These X-rays look great,' Hamish was saying when she arrived. He handed them over for Leesa to see.

'A great improvement,' Leesa concurred. 'The physio's report...' she quickly scanned the page of Mr Lewis's notes '...is very positive.'

'So there's no reason why you can't be transferred to the rehab hospital for further and more extensive physio for another week or so, before heading home.'

'Good news at last,' Mr Lewis responded. 'Although I am looking forward to returning home, I will miss all my new friends. Especially your family.'

'We'll all stay in touch,' Leesa told him firmly. She sneaked a glance at her watch. The place from which she'd ordered the food basket from was only down the street. The delivery should be here at any moment and she had to tell Janet and Angus what was going on.

'I'll be around next week to see how you're progressing,' Leesa told him quickly as she kept a close watch on the main corridor into the ward. 'And with the reports from the rehab doctors, we'll decide then when you can go home.'

'Thank you,' Mr Lewis replied.

Leesa checked the corridor once again. There was the delivery boy. He was here! He was walking down the corridor towards the nurses' station, a large wicker basket in his hands. Leesa felt a lump settle in her stomach as the nurse pointed him in the direction of room four.

'Isn't that right, Dr Stevenson?' Mr Lewis asked.

'Uh? Sorry,' Leesa quickly apologised, and turned her attention back to Mr Lewis.

'I was just saying that little Charlotte will be a big handful for her parents when they finally arrive home.'

'Uh…yes. Yes, she will, but I'm sure Janet's told you that both sets of parents will be back from overseas by then and they're all only too happy to play grandparents to their only grandchild.'

Leesa checked the corridor again and watched in horror as the delivery boy casually sauntered back up the corridor without the basket.

'Ah. Excuse me, Mr Lewis. I just have to…go and…do…er…something. Excuse me.' Leesa almost sprinted to room four but managed to control herself so as not to arouse too much suspicion.

There was still one nurse who was just finishing writing up Janet's chart when Leesa burst through the door.

Angus was lifting the red checked cloth that covered the basket and Leesa quickly crossed to him and slapped his hand away.

'Wait for everyone, Angus.'

'What? Who?' Angus spluttered, and Leesa simply gripped his hand a little tighter before he said, 'Oh, yes, of course. How rude of me.'

The nurse left the room with a puzzled frown on her face and would no doubt tell the rest of the staff that Dr Stevenson was acting very strangely indeed.

'It will probably add credence to the pregnancy rumour,' Leesa muttered crossly to herself.

'Who's pregnant?' Janet asked.

'And who sent this basket of goodies to us?' Angus questioned as he tried once more to raise the cloth.

Leesa slapped his hand again. 'It's not for you,' she told

him. 'And I'm the one who's supposedly pregnant,' she
told her sister.

'What?' They both said together.

'Oh, shush. Quickly. Hide the basket before Hamish
comes in and I'll explain everything.'

There weren't a lot of things in the sparse room behind
which to hide a large wicker basket so Leesa placed it in
the corner of the room behind Angus's bedside locker.
Hopefully, if Hamish didn't completely enter the room, he
wouldn't see it.

'Not a word to him,' she ordered both of them, before
he walked into the room.

'Are you feeling all right, Leesa?' Hamish asked with
concern.

'Of course I am,' she said a little too quickly. 'I…
um…just remembered something I had to do. It's done
now.' She gave him a sweet smile and he frowned at her.
'I'm just saying goodnight to these two.' She indicated
Janet and Angus, still smiling sweetly at Hamish.

He stopped frowning. 'Fine. I'll say goodnight as well.
I have a desk full of paperwork waiting for me.' He gave
Janet a kiss on the cheek and went to walk around the bed
to hug his brother but Leesa stood in the way, not letting
him pass. If he went around the bed, he'd definitely see the
basket.

Leesa quickly moved Janet's bedside table out of the way
so Hamish could squeeze past between the two beds. He
hugged his brother and gave Leesa another puzzled look.

'See you both tomorrow,' he said. 'And I'll see you
later.' He nodded in Leesa's direction, before walking out
of the room.

Janet let the giggles start the instant he left the room.

'Shh.' Leesa held up her hand and crept to the door. She
peeked around it to see Hamish leaving the ward. 'Whew!
OK, sis. Laugh all you want.'

'What's going on?' Angus asked. 'Who's the basket for?'

'It's for Hamish and myself.'

'I see,' he replied with dawning realisation. 'Planning a little…evening picnic in the moonlight?'

'Something like that.' Leesa shrugged.

'Does Hamish know?' Janet asked.

'He knows the time and the place but the basket's a surprise.'

Angus leaned back against his pillows. 'You do realise it will cost you to keep us silent?'

'Yes,' agreed Janet, after a brief look at her husband.

'All right. All right,' Leesa agreed. 'What do you want?'

'What else? A basket of goodies!' Angus folded his arms across his chest and smiled at his sister-in-law.

'Fine. I'll have it delivered tomorrow.'

'Don't you think it might look strange that two baskets arrive on two consecutive days?' Angus queried.

'You could be right,' Janet added. 'I think *you* should personally oversee the delivery of our basket—that way it might not attract so much attention.'

'Fine,' Leesa agreed.

'Good.' Janet smiled. 'Now we can move onto the next topic for discussion. Why are you pregnant?'

'I'm *not*,' Leesa said, and gritted her teeth. 'It's a rumour I've heard. Ever since Hamish and I were caught kissing in his office last Friday, the grapevine has been buzzing like a hive full of bees.'

'Well, it's about time you confessed that piece of gossip, although I did pick up on a few things the nurses have been saying.'

'We hadn't heard the pregnancy rumour, though,' Angus added. 'We'll do our best to squash that one.'

'So how is Hamish taking the gossip?'

'Not good but not bad either. We're basically not allowed to have contact—other than professional, of course—anywhere within a ten-mile radius of the hospital grounds.'

'Separate cars to work?' Angus asked.

'Definitely,' Leesa replied. 'So between that and being at home with Charlotte and Gabby—not that we're complaining,' she added quickly. 'We haven't had any time alone—really alone—for a few days.'

'So you thought you'd arrange a lovers' tryst.' Janet sighed. 'How romantic.'

'I must say, Leesa, that since Hamish has admitted to having feelings for you it's improved him no end. So, on behalf of my wife, myself and both sets of parents, we say thank you.'

'Yeah, yeah.' Leesa smiled at her brother-in-law and came around the bed to hug him. 'Now all I have to do is to somehow smuggle this basket out of the ward without it looking suspicious.'

'That's easy,' Angus announced. 'The next time one of the nurses comes in, we'll simply tell her you've taken the food home to freeze because we're both on a strict hospital-food-only diet—as ordered by our doctors.'

'Good idea.' Leesa smiled and collected the basket. 'Then I won't need to deliver tomorrow's basket here at all—I can just take it home and freeze it for you.'

'Ah, yes.' Angus frowned. 'I'd forgotten about that.'

'Tell you what,' Janet suggested. 'Why don't you wait until we arrive home and *then* have a basket of goodies delivered to us?'

'And it had better be twice as big as this basket,' Angus pointed out.

'Deal!' Leesa said with a laugh. 'Now I'd better get going. I have a few more things to organise.'

She said her goodbyes and carried the basket out of the ward, calling a cheery goodnight to the nurses as she went.

Put the gossip behind you, she told herself as she quickly stopped at her office to collect her bag and keys.

Concentrate on sharing a peaceful and romantic evening with the man you love.

Leesa drove back to her apartment so she could shower. She stood in front of her wardrobe for quite a while, trying to decide exactly what to wear, and finally settled on a black cotton dress that had thin straps and a short skirt. It showed off her legs and, since Hamish appeared to love her legs, the dress was simply perfect.

She applied a minimal amount of make-up and left her hair loose, its golden length flowing around her shoulders, tantalising her skin. Small, square diamond earrings finished off the outfit and Leesa twirled in front of her mirror.

'Get ready to take some deep breaths, Hamish, my love, because here I come!'

CHAPTER EIGHT

LEESA parked her car in the parking bay and waited for Hamish. She was a few minutes early and now spent her time fidgeting and constantly scanning the road for his car. Everything had to be perfect, she told herself for the hundredth time. A romantic picnic as they softly talked about a variety of topics that interested them. She sighed wistfully, eager to begin her evening alone with Hamish.

About three minutes later a car headed in her direction, causing her heart rate to increase she was so excited.

He parked his Jag next to her car. Leesa scrambled from the car, then forced herself to stop and take a few deep breaths so that she could walk to his car with unhurried poise and charm.

A smile lit his face as he came towards her. They stopped where they met, between the two cars, and Hamish brought his hands up to cup her face.

'You look...beautiful.'

'Thank you.' Leesa's joy overflowed and she threw her arms around his neck, bringing his head down so their lips could finally have contact.

Their mutual need for each other only seemed to increase as time progressed. The evidence was in the kiss they now shared—familiar, fervent and fiery.

Hamish slowly raised his head and smiled down at Leesa. 'My addiction for you appears to be getting worse.'

'Good.' She returned his smile and broke from the embrace. 'Shall we go for a little stroll through King Edward Park?'

He hesitated, but only for a moment. 'It appears you have your heart set on it.'

131

'Great. I just need to get something from my car.' Leesa collected the basket.

'You have been busy with your planning, haven't you?'

'I'm a woman of many talents,' she replied, as he took the basket from her and placed an arm about her shoulders.

'I'm beginning to realise that. So,' he asked as they walked towards the park, 'where did this basket spring from?'

'A shop.'

'Does it have anything to do with you acting strangely this afternoon?'

'It has *everything* to do with it.' She explained what had happened and how Janet and Angus had teased her.

Hamish chose a spot under a large Norfolk Island pine tree and spread the rug she'd placed on top of the basket. 'I guess that means they know about us.'

'Hamish, they're our family. They saw the changes in you long before I or anyone else said anything.'

'Meaning they've also heard the gossip from the staff.'

'I think it's also a case that they've been pumped for information by hospital personnel. Believe it or not, your younger brother and my older sister aren't as stupid as you might have suspected. They can put two and two together.' Leesa started unpacking the food.

'Mmm, looks delicious,' he murmured.

'Good, because I want us to relax and just enjoy being together.'

Hamish looked around the park, which had a few people strolling here and there, but for the most part it was quite deserted compared to a sunny weekend afternoon when it was hard to find a place to sit.

'Relax, I said,' Leesa ordered. 'I know you don't want anyone from the hospital to see us together but try to forget about the hospital—for a few hours. *Please?*'

'I'll try,' he replied as she handed him a plate of food.

They ate the delicious salads, cold chicken, cheese and

pâté, along with a glass of chilled white wine as they leisurely watched the night sky appear.

'Looks like another beautiful evening and another sunny
day tomorrow,' Leesa remarked as she packed everything
away. 'I must confess that I quite like daylight saving.
Being able to finish working at the hospital late and still
enjoy a good sunset is something to treasure.'

'You're an incurable romantic, aren't you?' he said as
he folded up the rug. He placed a brief kiss on her lips.
'I've known it for years, and the sad part is I've never felt
it. Thank you for sharing it with me.

Leesa's love for him threatened to rise up and overwhelm
her completely at his words. 'Let's take the basket back to
the car and go to the Bogey Hole.'

'You have this evening planned down to the last detail
and I, for one, am not going to spoil it. Lead on.'

'I've always loved the Bogey Hole,' Leesa said as she
held his hand after they'd left the picnic remains in her car.
She walked down the steps that led to the swimming hole
which was cut in a large rectangular shape in the rock at
the base of the cliff. A rusty old chain surrounded the
swimming hole as waves crashed against the rock ledge,
filling the pool with fresh sea water.

'General Whitlesea was a genius but, then, I guess when
you're the commanding officer at Fort Scratchley and you
want somewhere private to bathe, why not have your own
pool built for you. *And* he was able to bathe in fresh sea
water.'

'With all of its charms,' Hamish scoffed. 'Seaweed, plas-
tic bags, even the odd shoe.'

'You're such a cynic,' she remarked with a laugh as she
slipped off her shoes and walked to the edge of the pool
where the water was gently lapping. 'It's lovely and warm.'

Hamish stood on the steps and looked down at her. 'Be
careful.'

'I intend to be.'

Hamish watched as she stood there, her eyes closed, her loose blonde hair being blown back by the soft breeze. The edge of her black dress fluttered around the top of her thighs and he felt his gut twist in a now familiar way as he perused her long and luscious legs.

He knew she was even more in love with him than she'd been for the past few years, and although he didn't want to hurt her he knew it was inevitable. It was the reason he'd maintained his distance for so long. After his disastrous marriage, there was no way he'd ever walk down the aisle again.

She turned her head slightly and opened her eyes, the dark pools of blue surrounding her pupils beckoning to him.

'I guess I can't persuade you to join me, can I?'

'Sorry,' he said with a slight shake of his head, a small smile on his lips. Leesa looked at him for another second. She knew that look in his eyes. It was the big-brother look but mingled with desire. The poor man still didn't know which way was up but she knew that, given time, she would be able to guide him through the perplexity of emotions he was now experiencing.

Leesa carefully and slowly made her way back to him. He reached out a hand and she took it for support.

'There now. No harm done.'

'That's what *you* think?' he muttered, and brought her close to him for a hard and longing kiss. 'Do you have any idea how incredibly captivating you are?'

'I guess not, but I think you should tell me.'

Hamish brought his mouth down for another kiss, one hand still holding hers, his other arm circling her waist to draw her closer. His lips on hers were seeking and demanding, and Leesa willingly gave everything she had. He deepened the kiss, holding her tightly to him, his hand squeezing hers as though he never wanted to let her go.

Finally he broke free, his ragged breathing echoing hers.

In his eyes, Leesa saw passionate desire but concern at the same time.

'Slowly,' she whispered to him, and gently eased back. 'Ready for the next part of the evening?'

He raked a hand through his hair, revealing his attempt to gain control over his emotions once more.

'Am I allowed to ask what it entails?'

Leesa smiled. 'Aren't you going to trust me?' They walked back up the steps and headed for their cars. A group of rowdy teenage boys had just pulled up and were hurrying, towels slung over their naked shoulders, down towards the Bogey Hole.

'I've behaved myself so far,' Hamish said as he looked over his shoulder at the boys, before turning his attention back to Leesa. 'Don't I get rewarded for good behaviour?'

'All right. The next part of my plan is to take you back to my apartment so we can sit outside on my very small but very private balcony and do some star-gazing.'

Hamish stopped beside her car. 'Do you think that's a good idea?'

'As you said, you've behaved yourself so far and we did agree to take it slowly. The point of this evening, Hamish, is romance. Most people scoff at it and others think it's dead—but not me. You know I'm an incurable romantic— you said so yourself. I'm not talking about sex. Allow me to help you *feel* what romance is all about.'

She leaned back against the car and Hamish's body seemed intent on following hers. Leesa put her arms around his neck as he leaned against her. 'Trust me, Hamish.' She urged his head down so their lips could meet, but when they were only a breath away they heard a loud, blood-curdling scream.

'Those boys,' Hamish muttered. 'Get your medical bag out of the car,' he called as he raced down towards the swimming hole.

It only took Leesa a second to do as he'd directed, and

by the time she arrived Hamish was at the bottom of the steps, helping three boys get their unconscious friend out of the water before he drowned.

'I—I told him not to do it,' stammered one of the boys, who had short, spiky blond hair. 'I told Simon he'd get hurt.'

'Is that his name?' Hamish queried.

'Yeah. Simon. Simon Watson. I'm Dave, this is Tom and Rob.' He gestured with his head to the twin brothers, one with long reddish hair and the other with his reddish locks short and spiked.

They dragged Simon up onto the edge where Leesa had been standing previously. She rushed over and knelt beside the boy.

'He's not breathing,' she stated, as she pushed his long blond locks from across his face. Hamish helped her turn him on his side so she could clear his airway before she tipped his head back, pinched his nose and began breathing into his mouth.

Hamish performed cardiopulmonary resuscitation before Leesa again breathed into Simon's mouth, his chest rising as she filled his lungs with air. Seconds later, he spluttered and coughed.

Once again they tipped Simon onto his side so he could cough up the water he'd swallowed. The boy opened his eyes briefly and gazed at Leesa, his vision glassy, as though he weren't seeing her at all, before his lids shuttered closed and he slipped back into unconsciousness.

'Tell me exactly what happened,' Hamish ordered Dave, as he and the other boys sat by, frightened looks on all their faces.

'You guys are real doctors, aren't you?' Dave asked with a worried expression on his face.

'Yes,' Hamish replied a little quickly. 'Tell me what happened.'

'He wanted to jump from that rock up there but we told him not to. Simon's a real daredevil and wouldn't listen.'

'Yeah,' agreed Rob. 'He's always showing off.'

Hamish listened while he ran his hands over the boy's limbs, checking for broken bones. Leesa pulled her torch from the bag and checked Simon's eyes, then his pulse.

'Which rock?' Hamish asked. They all looked to where the three boys pointed. It was quite a way up and Simon could have easily been killed.

'Fractured metatarsals and tarsals on both sides, fractured right rib, definite concussion—and I'd like to have his spine X-rayed along with the other areas.'

'Pupils are fine, pulse is racing.'

'Let's get these injuries splinted and bandaged so he's ready to be moved when the ambulance arrives. Do you have your phone in the bag?' Hamish asked.

'No. It's in the car.' Leesa fished out her keys and handed them to Dave. 'The blue Mazda 121. My phone should be in the glovebox. Switch it on—the unlock code is seven, three, seven, zero—then dial triple zero for an ambulance. Give them our location and tell them there are doctors in attendance. Then call Simon's parents and have them meet us at Newcastle General's Emergency Department. Got it?'

'Yes,' Dave replied, and took the steps two at a time, causing Leesa to hold her breath until he made it safely to the top.

They monitored Simon, bandaging his injuries and elevating them as best they could, as well as keeping him warm with the towels so he wouldn't go into shock. Leesa inspected the lump on Simon's head where he'd obviously hit the side of the pool. There was only a small amount of blood, which would eventually require sutures, but for now she applied a pressure bandage.

'A few sutures will fix the split in his head but he'll still require an X-ray,' she remarked to Hamish. 'How are you two holding up?' she asked Tom and Rob, who were sitting down on the bottom step, hugging their knees to their chests.

'Yeah, we're fine. We were just saying we should'a made Simon listen to us. We should'a stopped him—but we didn't.'

'Without wanting to sound too much like a grown-up,' Hamish said as he took off his wet shoes and rolled up the bottom of his wet trousers, 'You've all learned a valuable and important lesson today. It's not worth taking uncalculated risks. Apply this new-found wisdom to everything you do.'

'Man, I don't know what we would've done if you both hadn't been here.'

'Then perhaps you should enrol in a first-aid course,' Leesa suggested with a sweet smile that caused both boys to immediately smile back and nod enthusiastically.

Dave returned, accompanied by the ambulance team. The paramedics performed their job with professional attention and soon Simon was on his way to the hospital. Hamish had suggested that the other boys go home and try to relax. They could see their friend tomorrow. Both Leesa and Hamish followed—each in their own car.

After the ambulance had pulled up outside the emergency department, Hamish and Leesa parked their cars to the side of the emergency bay.

'Give me your keys.' Hamish held out his hand to Leesa who handed over her keys as they both rushed into Casualty.

'Park our cars.' He gave the keys to an orderly before they followed Simon into a treatment room.

'Mr O'Donnell,' the triage sister said with surprise. 'Are you on call this evening?'

'Not that I know of,' he replied as he and Leesa attended to Simon. 'We attended this boy at the accident site. Bogey Hole—the paramedics have the report. I need X-rays of both feet, antero-posterior views of tibia, spinal column and skull, stat.'

'Yes, Doctor,' the triage sister replied as she took notes.

'His parents have been contacted and should be arriving soon. Leesa, take care of the X-ray arrangements. I'll go speak to Theatre Sister about my requirements.' With that he walked off and Leesa headed over to the sister's desk to fill out the request forms for Radiology.

'You look…nice, Leesa,' Roberta McNeil, who had been Triage Sister in Casualty for the past five years, said.

'Thanks.' Leesa concentrated on the task at hand, trying her hardest to ignore any innuendos in the other woman's voice.

'So, have you and the handsome Hamish been enjoying each other's company this evening? After all, if you hadn't, how could *both* of you have attended the teenager?'

When Leesa remained silent, Roberta continued, 'The Bogey Hole is so lovely and romantic, especially as the sun sets and the night sky appears.'

Leesa cringed inwardly, sincerely thankful Hamish wasn't around to hear this. Then again, she doubted whether Roberta would have had the guts to say *anything* while Hamish had been in Casualty.

So why did that mean that *she* always caught the speculative glances, the edges of gossip and the probing questions? She thought about what track she should take in this instance. She'd promised Hamish to remain discreet and that included not talking to such a gossip as Roberta about her private life.

However, if she ignored Roberta's questions completely, it would only give more credence to the rumours the other woman would spread. On the other hand, she could play Roberta's own game, seeing she'd witnessed a kiss a few weeks previously between the triage sister and the very married head of neurology. But then she'd be no better than Roberta herself. Realising that it wouldn't matter what she did or didn't say, Roberta would gossip about it regardless, Leesa stood and gathered up the completed paperwork.

'I'll go around to Radiology with Simon and stay with him while he has his X-rays. Who's the anaesthetist on call?'

'Pete Farrell.'

'Good,' Leesa responded, and started to walk away. She stopped, turned and walked back to Roberta, a fake smile pasted in place. Roberta's smugness seemed to wane a little as Leesa said softly, 'I'm not in favour of hospital gossip, as I'm sure you'd agree, but if people want to continue to speculate on whatever, if anything, may or may not be happening between Hamish and myself, then that's their perrogative. Better they talk about us than *other* people.' Leesa watched as Roberta's jaw dropped and her face flushed crimson. Taking pity on the other woman, Leesa placed her hand on Roberta's shoulder and said sincerely, 'Be careful.'

Roberta bit her bottom lip as it started to quiver and tears welled in her eyes. She nodded at Leesa's words, then said shakily, 'I think I'll take my teabreak now.'

'Sure. Don't worry about Simon Watson. I'll arrange for an orderly to wheel him to Radiology.'

'OK, and…uh…thanks, Leesa.' Roberta quickly turned and walked away. Leesa breathed a sigh of relief. She wasn't quite sure what Roberta had thanked her for. Was it for not saying anything about the kiss she'd witnessed? For pointing out that gossiping was wrong and hurtful? Or for organising an orderly to take Simon Watson to Radiology?

She gave her head a little shake and continued with her job.

The radiographs showed several broken bones in both feet—namely three toes on the right and two on the left, as well as a fracture to the right heel, fractured right tibia, but no damage to the skull or spine. At worst-case scenario, the coccyx at the base of the spine was more than likely very bruised.

'Here's Dr Stevenson now,' Roberta announced as Leesa made her way through Casualty, intent on delivering the X-rays to Hamish for his opinion. She stopped and Roberta introduced her to Mr and Mrs Watson, Simon's parents. Both of them had grey hair and Leesa guessed them to be in their late fifties or early sixties. She was a little surprised as she'd assumed his parents would be much younger.

'We believe you were with our son straight after the accident happened?' Mr Watson asked as his wife wiped the tears from her eyes.

'Yes. Mr O'Donnell, the surgeon who will be operating on Simon, and I were both nearby when it happened. If you'd like to come with me to the family waiting room I'll get Mr O'Donnell for you and we can explain what happened.'

'Thank you.' Mr Watson smiled.

His wife reached out and placed her hand on Leesa's arm, her expression intent. 'Is he going to be all right?'

'Yes.' Leesa nodded for emphasis. 'Because he received prompt attention, he'll be fine. Come with me and we'll explain everything.'

'Hospital admission forms have been signed,' Roberta said, handing Leesa the casenotes.

'Thanks, Roberta,' Leesa said as she showed the Watsons the way.

After leaving them in the waiting room and showing them how the tea- and coffee-making facilities worked, Leesa continued on her way to find Hamish. He was standing in the receiving bay, talking with Pete.

'Here they are.' She held out the packet of X-rays to Hamish. 'Hi, Pete. The patient's back in Cas if you want to review him. His parents are in the waiting room.'

'Thanks, Leesa. Has he regained consciousness yet?'

'Yes. Just as we were leaving Radiology, so my guess is he's ready for some pain relief.'

'Right. I'll give him his pre-med and see you both in Theatre.'

They watched him go and Hamish quickly ushered Leesa into the doctors' tearoom where they could be alone.

'What's the matter?' she asked as he hooked the radiographs onto the viewing machine.

'Nothing. I just wondered how things went in Casualty.'

'Fine. Why are you checking up—?

'Not with the patient—with the staff. Both of us coming in together. Both of us being there when the boy had his accident. I caught Triage Sister trying to hide her smiles. Did she give you a hard time?'

'Hamish.' Leesa smiled. 'I'm a big girl now. Remember?'

'Stop reminding me. It's been uppermost in my mind for the past month or so. You're a grown woman and you don't need me as a big brother, but that doesn't stop me from caring about whether people hurt your feelings or not.'

'That's sweet,' she said, her eyes shining her love for him. She forced herself to maintain her distance, even though she itched to hold his hand or put her arms around him or kiss him. 'Yes, she did say something and, no, she didn't hurt me and, yes, I took care of the situation, hopefully, ensuring she won't be spreading any more gossip for quite some time.'

He gave her a frown. 'What on earth did you say to her?'

'Not much. Let it go. Have a look at the X-rays and then we can go speak to his parents.'

Hamish crossed to her side and placed his hands on her shoulders. 'You're great.' He smiled at her and started to lean towards her for a kiss.

'Stop!' She placed one hand on his chest and gently pushed him away. 'It's against the rules to fraternise with your research fellow in hospital grounds.'

'So it is.' His smile increased and he turned his attention back to the radiographs. 'Three broken metatarsals on the right and two on the left, as well as a small fracture to the calcaneus on the right. We'll strap both feet from ankle down. His right tibia is another matter. The fracture is impacted, which will mean wiring the small pieces of bone back together. Thank goodness his spine appears fine, as does the skull.'

He turned to face Leesa. 'That boy has had a lucky escape and I sincerely hope he realises it.'

'Let's go and discuss this with his parents.'

'How are they?' he asked as he replaced the X-rays into the packet.

'Shaken up, understandably.'

Leesa and Hamish explained exactly what had happened to Simon and showed his parents the radiographs.

'So those are the procedures we'll be performing now,' Hamish finished.

'It all...sounds...easy enough,' Mr Watson mumbled. 'Not that I'll pretend to understand completely what you've said.'

'He's always been a wild child,' Mrs Watson said softly as she gave them a watery smile. 'He was a late surprise for us. Our other children are all married with children of their own. I had Simon just after I'd turned forty. Ever since he got his driver's license a few months ago, he's been even more reckless.'

'We tend to spoil him a bit more now that he's our only child at home,' Mr Watson added.

'If anything were to happen to him...' Mrs Watson broke off, fresh tears gathering in her eyes.

'He'll be fine,' Hamish stated clearly.

'If you don't have any further questions,' Leesa said as she handed Mr Watson a hospital permission form, 'we need you to read and sign this. As Simon is only seventeen,

you're still his legal guardians. If you need anything explained, let me know.'

Hamish looked at his watch. 'If you'll excuse me, I'll go
and get ready for Theatre.'

'Thank you,' Mr Watson said, and held out a hand to
Hamish. 'For everything.'

Hamish nodded. 'We'll see you after the surgery.'

Leesa went through the permission details and the rest
of the hospital's protocols. 'He'll be an inpatient for at least
a week, depending on how well he recovers. The bandages
around his feet will need to be on for at least six to eight
weeks and he'll be in a wheelchair during that time as he
won't be allowed to bear weight while the bones knit back
together.

'Once he's out of Theatre and settled in the ward, you
might want to collect some personal items for him and
bring them in. Pyjamas or clothes, toothbrushes, combs—
personal effects. The hospital does have an emergency kit
that our volunteers make up which contains a razor, face-
washers, toothbrush, toothpaste and other things so he'll be
fine for the moment.'

There was a knock at the door and Pete Farrell walked
in. He introduced himself to Simon's parents.

'I've just given him some pain relief and the nursing staff
are currently preparing him for Theatre. He's a healthy lad
and should have no trouble at all with the anaesthetic.' His
beeper sounded and he quickly looked at the number.

'It's Theatre so we should be going, Leesa.'

Leesa stood up. 'As I said before, help yourselves to tea
and coffee. There are snack-vending machines out in
Casualty foyer and the hospital cafeteria is on level five.
Just ask one of the staff out in Cas how to get there and
they'll help you. We'll be a few hours at least but, remember, he'll be fine.'

'Thank you,' Mr Watson said, and shook hands with

both of them. 'We just can't thank you enough for what you're doing for our boy.'

'Let's get moving,' Pete said, and waited for Leesa to precede him out of the small room.

The operation proceeded without a hitch, although it did take Hamish and Leesa slightly longer than anticipated to fix the tibia back together. The small bony fragments required fiddling to position correctly, but with determination and persistence they were soon closing the wound. Hamish gave the signal for Pete to reverse the anaesthetic.

Once out of Theatre, Leesa and Hamish gave Simon's parents the good news as their son was taken to Recovery.

'You'll be able to see him soon,' Leesa told them. 'We'll arrange for someone to take you to the ward and we'll be around to check on him tomorrow morning.'

'Who will look after him during the night?' Mrs Watson asked with concern.

'The nursing staff will be there and one of the orthopaedic registrars will be on duty. He's been given pethidine for the pain and will more than likely sleep through the night,' Leesa assured them.

'He has an intravenous drip which will not only be keeping his body fluids at a normal level but also carries a dose of antibiotics to stave off any infection.' Hamish nodded. 'He'll be fine.'

They changed out of their theatre clothes and prepared to go home. Hamish collected both sets of keys from the orderlies' station and they walked out to the doctors' car park. Hamish followed Leesa's car back to Janet's and Angus's house and parked behind her in the driveway.

'So much for a nice romantic evening alone,' he murmured, placing his arm about her shoulders.

Leesa smiled up at him. 'At least we were together,' she rationalised.

'Being in Theatre, with staff all around us and a patient between us, isn't really my idea of togetherness.'

Leesa laughed and kissed him quickly, before collecting her briefcase and the basket from the back of the car. Hamish gathered up his things and they headed for the door. They quietly let themselves inside as the grandfather clock in the front room chimed midnight. Putting their things down, Leesa went into his open arms and snuggled up against his chest.

'You don't seem to realise that I don't care where we are, Hamish, as long as we can be together.'

'I know.' He slowly eased her away from him. The expression on his face wasn't one of joy. Leesa frowned and eyed him warily.

'What's the matter?'

He raked a hand through his hair. 'Why don't you sit down? I have something to say.'

'I can take it standing up,' she told him, a terrible fear clutching at her heart. 'I thought we'd agreed what to do regarding the hospital gossip.'

'We did. That's not the problem.' He turned from her and paced around the room a little, something he always did when he was concerned.

'Out with it, Hamish.' He didn't speak. 'Don't you *like* spending time with me?'

'Yes,' he replied quickly. 'I do. I've fought the attraction between us for so long, and now that I don't have to I start to worry about you.'

'You mean about you breaking my heart.'

'Yes. How do you know?'

Her smile was sad. 'It's *me* you're talking to. The woman who's been in love with you for the past decade. Hamish, we're perfect for each other—don't you see? We're each the other's missing half.'

'Perhaps, but that doesn't change things.'

'What things?'

'The fact that, regardless of how perfect we are for each other or how good we are together, we can never be more than what we are.' He balled his hands into fists. 'This is why I was fighting the attraction between us for so long. Why I knew that if I ever gave in to it I'd end up hurting you, and I care about you far too much to ever intentionally hurt you.'

'What are you talking about?' The question was asked softly, although Leesa was almost sure she knew the answer before it came.

'Marriage, Leesa. I've tried it once and it didn't work. Marriage just isn't for me.' He stopped pacing and took her hands in his. 'Regardless of what I feel for you—regardless of how much I don't want to hurt you—I know that I will and it's been eating away at me.'

'You *can't* marry me or you *won't* marry me?' She forced her voice to remain calm, knowing that hysteria would only make matters worse.

'Both.' His answer was like a bullet through the heart.

CHAPTER NINE

LEESA extracted her hands from Hamish's and calmly crossed to sit in a comfortable chair.

'Why don't you tell me about it?'

'What?' he asked as he slumped down beside her.

'Your marriage to Sandra.' She spoke the words softly, knowing the only course of action open to her now was to trust her heart. She'd always known that she and Hamish would be together and, regardless of his words, she still knew it to be true.

'Now?' He pointedly looked at his watch.

'Yes. We're both used to living on no sleep, but the sooner you start, the sooner you'll be finished.'

'What would you like to know?'

'Let's start with how you met. I don't remember much except that your parents were very surprised by your actions.' She shrugged when he glared at her. 'What? I was still in high school. Even if I'd wanted to find out what happened, our parents would stop talking about it the instant I entered the room.'

'Great. Thanks for pointing out the eleven-year age difference between us. You make me feel so old.'

'I'm not pointing anything out—I'm simply stating the facts. Besides, the difference in our ages is not the issue here.'

'Leesa, getting me to talk about my marriage isn't going to achieve anything. I won't change my mind.'

'I'm not asking you to. I'm simply asking you to tell me what happened.' She waited patiently for him to speak.

'It was a mistake from the beginning,' he finally said with a hint of reluctance. 'We were friends throughout medical school, and after we'd finished our internship Sandra suggested we get married.'

'Why?' Leesa queried softly. 'Did you suspect she was pregnant?'

'No,' he stated bluntly.

'I'm not criticising, Hamish, I'm merely trying to understand. Why did she suggest you get married?'

He stood and began to pace the room. She watched him walk up and down a few times, his jaw rigid as he remembered what had transpired. Then he stopped, faced her and ran a hand frustratedly through his hair.

'It was just the type of crazy, spontaneous thing that Sandra did. She was always like that. After spending hours at the hospital, studying and working, she'd suggest we drive to Sydney—simply for a cup of coffee. Mind you, it was usually around three o'clock in the morning. There was a group of us and Sandra was the ringleader. Regardless of what she suggested, she generally had to talk me into going.

'She'd constantly tell me to loosen up. To relax. To live a little. So I did and I had to admit that sometimes it was fun. But most of the time I felt as though I had to watch out for her. That if I didn't go along, she'd do something really stupid. I was more easily persuaded in those days. I know offering immaturity as an excuse appears weak but that was the case.'

He began pacing again and Leesa clenched her hands tighter together in her lap. It was more difficult than she'd imagined—hearing Hamish speak of his relationship with his ex-wife—but she constantly had to remind herself that it had all happened a long time ago. Now it would be her turn to persuade Hamish to do something—to let the past go and live in the present. Yet now he wasn't so easy to persuade.

'When she suggested we get married, it was simply another one of her spontaneous ideas. I didn't take her seriously until she obtained the forms and filled them in, coax-

ing me to sign them. Sandra was such an optimist—
everything would turn out right. We loved each other,
didn't we? So why not shock everyone with a secret marriage and play house? She said it would be fun. Her ar-
guments were so convincing and I thought if we did go
ahead with it, she would calm down—settle down and stop
doing the wild and crazy things she'd always done.'

. He sat down on the coffee-table and looked intently at
Leesa. 'I was wrong. It wasn't fun at all. In fact, things
were worse than ever. My parents were disappointed in me,
even though I was a grown man. I remember my mother
simply looking at me and shaking her head sadly. She told
me I had always had good judgement but this was one time
when she didn't agree with me. That was all she said, and
she was so right. I was twenty-five and thought myself so
grown and mature, but I hadn't remained true to myself.'

He leaned forward and took Leesa's hand in his. 'The
marriage was a nightmare. Sandra would be out until all
hours, still doing her crazy things, but now she wouldn't
even tell me where she was going. I was accepted onto the
service registrar rotation for Orthopaedics so I was working
longer hours at the hospital. Sandra wanted position and
money and couldn't understand why I wasn't content just
to become a general practitioner. She wanted us to run a
practice in an upmarket suburb of Sydney where we'd be
''raking in the money'', as she'd termed it.

'For a start, I had no interest in moving to Sydney or
anywhere else for that matter. I *wanted* to plant roots—to
carve out a career for myself in orthopaedics. Besides, I
like living in Newcastle.'

Leesa smiled at him. 'I know what you mean. I've
worked overseas and in Sydney but Newcastle is always
my home.'

Hamish didn't return her smile. 'Sandra went to
Melbourne for a conference and never came back. She left
a message on the answering machine, telling me she wasn't

having fun and that she was filing for a divorce.' He
dropped Leesa's hands and stood up.

'Not only had I failed in my marriage but I'd lost a
person whom I'd classified as a very close friend. My feelings for her were very strong—although I admitted to myself not long after I signed the divorce papers that I was
never really in love with her.'

'So you pushed all reminders of your marriage and your
"fall from grace" to the back of your mind, locked your
heart up and proceeded with your life,' Leesa said with
control. The anger she felt towards him was still bubbling
beneath the surface.

'Something like that.' His facial expression was bland—
the shutters were down. 'Would you like a cup of tea?'

The anger burst forth. 'No, Hamish.' Leesa stood. 'I
would *not* like a cup of tea. What I would like, though, is
for you to tell me *why* you won't marry *me*. I'm not the
least bit like Sandra—or haven't you realised that yet?'

'Of course I—'

'Then why?' she interrupted him. 'What's the problem?'
She faltered for a second, her voice not nearly as strong as
she'd have liked it to be when she said, 'Don't you love
me?'

He crossed to her side and placed his hands on her shoulders. 'Of course I do. Can't you see? That's the problem.'

Leesa stared up at him, a frown creasing her forehead.
This wasn't how she'd envisioned a declaration of love
from Hamish. She tried to clarify it.

'I don't mean love me as a sister but as a woman.'

'I know what you mean, Leesa, and, yes, I do love you
as a woman.' He cupped her face with one of his hands,
his voice now soft. 'A beautiful and desirable woman.' He
brushed his lips across hers for emphasis. 'A woman whose
intellect, dedication, persistence and friendship I admire
and value too highly to risk losing.'

Leesa stepped away from him, breaking all physical contact between them. 'Let me get this straight. You don't want to risk *losing* me by *marrying* me?'

'I know you're nothing like Sandra, but you are my closest friend. I lost a good friend in the past and it took me years to come to terms with it. I don't want the same thing to happen to us. I value your friendship too much. If we were married, the light that shines so brightly within you would fizzle out and die. I can't watch that happen to you. That's why I've tried to keep you at arm's length for so long. I knew I'd hurt you one way or the other.'

'Arrgghh,' Leesa said between clenched teeth and stamped her foot. 'Stop being so selfish!'

'I'm not being selfish,' he stated calmly.

Leesa looked at him. She knew if she stood there any longer, trying to debate this matter with him, she'd end up throttling him. She took a few deep breaths, before saying calmly, 'I'm going to bed.'

Thankfully he made no effort to stop her—or kiss her goodnight. Up in her bedroom, Leesa went through her night-time routine quickly, still angry and frustrated.

'He's just so stubborn.' She pounded the pillow beside her. Receiving the admission that he loved her, instead of making all her dreams come true as she'd believed for years, had brought numbness instead.

She concentrated on deep-breathing exercises, knowing she must formulate a new plan. Finally, her pulse rate began to return to normal as she laid back on the pillows, the ceiling fan above her whirring softly as she closed her eyes.

So Hamish admired her intellect, her dedication and her persistence, did he?

'Fine!' she said out loud. She'd show him just how smart, dedicated and persistent she could be, especially now she knew he loved her.

Simon Watson was sitting up in bed, eating a light breakfast, when Leesa and Hamish did their ward round the next morning. The teenager smiled shyly at Leesa.

'My mates told me you saved my life. You know, mouth to mouth an' all that.' His eyes were alight with infatuation.

Leesa smiled warmly at him. 'Have your friends been in already?'

Simon responded to her smile, his own growing wider. 'Yeah. They wanted to catch some early waves so they dropped in before school.'

'You've had a lucky escape,' Hamish said sternly as they perused his chart. 'I gather you won't go doing anything so foolish again.'

'Ah, no, Doc. No, I won't,' Simon said, the smile disappearing from his face.

'Glad to hear it. How's the pain?'

'Can't feel a thing,' Simon said, his smile returning as he looked at Leesa again. 'Besides, I can cope with a bit of pain.'

'I think you've coped with enough for now,' she said firmly, her smile still in place. 'Please, tell the nurses if the pain increases. It's normal for the injuries you've sustained.'

'Uh—yeah. OK, then. I'll tell the nurses.'

'Good.'

'Ready to move on, Dr Stevenson?' Hamish said sharply from behind her. 'We do have other patients to see as well as an operation to get through this morning.'

'You concentrate on getting better,' Leesa said with a smile as they moved on to the next patient. They finished the ward round and, after saying a brief hello to Janet and Angus, Leesa and Hamish made their way to the theatre block.

'I'll thank you not to flirt with the patients,' Hamish said as they walked side by side towards the changing rooms.

'As you wish,' she acknowledged. 'I'll thank you to remember you're in love with me—but won't do anything about it—and to hide your jealousy better in future.' She pushed the door open to the female changing rooms and disappeared inside before he could retaliate.

She grinned at her reflection, proud of the way she was handling him. When she'd woken that morning, he'd been gone. There had been an empty teacup, rinsed and placed in the dishwasher, which she'd presumed had been his, indicating he had at least slept at his brother's house the previous night. She wouldn't have blamed him if he'd moved back into his apartment, but Angus had asked him to stay and Hamish was a man of his word.

'Hi, Leesa,' Caroline Metcalfe said as she entered the changing rooms. 'I'd heard you were doing a case on Mr Tindall's list.'

'That's right.' Leesa smiled.

Caroline hesitated for a moment. 'You're in a good mood.' She lowered her voice and said softly, 'Does it have anything to do with the head of orthopaedics?'

Leesa's smile grew. 'Everything.'

'Great. So things are going fine, are they?'

'Not really, but I haven't spent half my life being in love with the man to let a minor setback worry me.'

Caroline laughed. 'Good to hear it. Go get him.'

'That's how I feel sometimes. As though I'm hunting the poor man but he's just so…' Leesa clenched her hands into fists and Caroline nodded.

'He's just so typically male. I know, they can be very frustrating.'

The two women finished changing and went to the scrub room. Mrs Leonard was in the receiving bay and Leesa stopped to see how she was doing.

'Feeling groggy,' her patient said as she tried to keep her eyes open.

'That's to be expected, Mrs Leonard. Just close your eyes and relax. Mr O'Donnell and I will take care of everything.'

Once the operation was under way, Leesa and Hamish

worked as the professionals they were. From years of experience, she anticipated what he would need and when, allowing the surgery to be completed on time.

If anyone in the theatre noticed the slight coolness in their chief surgeon, no one mentioned it, although the way he continually referred to Leesa as Dr Stevenson, instead of Leesa, was bound to give the gossipers more ammunition for the rumour mill.

Look on the bright side, she told herself as she changed out of her theatre garb back into her navy linen shorts and white knit top. At least the rumour concerning her alleged pregnancy would be discarded.

During the afternoon, Leesa concentrated on her research work, writing up notes and calling patients. As the study was on long bones, she paid a visit to her brother-in-law to talk him into volunteering.

'I don't know if I want to be a guinea pig,' Angus retorted when she suggested it. She wasn't sure if he was teasing or not.

'Can I believe what I'm hearing?' Leesa asked. 'A fellow colleague and a member of my family *refusing* to assist in the advancement of medical science?'

'No,' he amended his reply, after a brief look at his wife.

Leesa looked across at Janet who was smiling sweetly. 'Of course Angus will be a part of your study. It must be difficult, finding people willing to co-operate. It's just that he's such a baby sometimes.'

'As I explained, I need to take X-rays and will ask you to fill in questionnaires.'

'Do I have to answer all the questions truthfully?' Angus asked, and this time Leesa knew he was teasing.

'Yes, or you'll have big brother to answer to.'

'Then I'll be honest,' he replied earnestly. 'Speaking of big brother, how's it going between the two of you?'

Leesa looked down at her hands as she answered, 'Not too good at the moment.'

'What happened?' Janet asked.

'Do you want me to talk to him?' Angus offered.

Leesa smiled at them both. 'It's all under control. I know how to handle Hamish.'

'So the romantic picnic didn't work out too well?' Angus asked the question.

'We heard about the teenage boy you brought in yesterday evening. The hospital grapevine was working overtime this morning,' Janet clarified.

'I'll just bet it was and they won't be finished with us by the time this day ends. Hamish was…rather cool to me in Theatre and it caused a few raised eyebrows.'

'What does the man think he's doing?' Angus growled. 'He's an idiot if he can't see what a great and wonderful person you are.'

'Excuse me?' Janet admonished her husband. 'It took you a while to realise the woman of your dreams was right in front of you. For a while there I thought I'd lost you for ever.'

'Yeah,' he agreed sheepishly. 'But I came to my senses in the end, didn't I? I married you, became a partner in the practice and had a child, didn't I?'

'And are you happy?' Janet asked softly, her love for her husband clearly in her eyes.

'Mrs O'Donnell, I'm ecstatic,' he replied, with desire burning in his eyes.

'I'll leave you two alone,' Leesa suggested, and went to the door. Angus called her name and she stopped.

'He'll come around.'

'Oh, I'm sure he will,' Leesa remarked. 'By the time I'm finished with your brother, he'll be as happy and as ecstatic as yourself.'

'That's what I like to hear,' Angus said with a laugh.

On Friday, Simon Watson was ready for discharge. Both his feet were still firmly strapped and he would be in a wheelchair for a few more weeks until they were properly healed.

'The check X-rays you had taken this morning,' Leesa told him, 'showed strong formation of bone callus, which means things are healing nicely. Your tibia still needs to be supported in the splint and you'll need to sit on a firm cushion to help with the bruising around the coccyx. That's the bone right at the base of your spine where you feel all that pain.'

Simon nodded and held out his hand. 'Thanks, Dr Stevenson,' he said. Leesa placed her hand into his and was surprised when he raised it to his lips for a brief kiss. She smiled at him.

'Promise me you'll do your exercises,' she said pointedly. 'I want good reports from your physiotherapist and your parents when I see you in clinic next week.'

'I promise.' He smiled up at her. 'So long as I get to see *you* in the clinic.'

She nodded. 'I'll make a note of it on the clinic list.'

Hamish cleared his throat and scowled at Leesa. She was hard pressed not to laugh out loud as it was the first sign of emotion he'd shown her all week long. Around the house he avoided her, and when they were together in the hospital he was aloof and professional.

'I hope you've learned from this experience,' Hamish said in an authoritative tone.

'Yes, Mr O'Donnell, I have,' Simon said, wiping the smile from his face.

'We'll take good care of him,' Mr Watson promised as he took hold of the wheelchair. He looked over his shoulder to where Mrs Watson had finished packing up Simon's things and was holding the bag.

'Right. Let's get you home, son.' With that, the Watson family left.

Hamish looked at Leesa, his jaw rigid, his scowl still in place. Because they were standing in the centre of the ward, he was unable to say anything to her. Besides, she saw nothing wrong with her conduct. If Simon Watson had taken a shine to her, she'd done absolutely nothing to encourage it. It was a crush, that was all and it wasn't the first time it had happened with a young male patient. Leesa was flattered by it and knew that within a few weeks she would be nothing but a distant memory to Simon Watson.

She smiled sweetly at Hamish before turning and walking to he women's ward, purposely swishing her hips as she went.

Mrs Leonard was progressing nicely and her physiotherapist was marvelling at her dedication towards exercising.

'I've told the young lassie that I've already had so many parts of me replaced I know the benefits exercise can provide.'

'You are definitely an expert, Mrs Leonard,' Leesa told her.

As the rest of the ward round team headed towards Mrs Leonard's bed, she quickly placed one of her frail and twisted hands on Leesa's and said, 'Can you slip back and see me when this circus is finished?'

Leesa nodded. 'I'll make the time.'

Throughout the rest of the ward round, Leesa was both a little worried and curious as to why Mrs Leonard wanted to see her.

'Aren't you coming to Theatre?' Hamish asked as she headed back to the women's part of the ward when their patient discussions were finished.

'Yes. Mrs Leonard asked to see me privately.'

'Don't take too long,' he warned, and left.

Leesa crossed to her patient's bedside.

'Pull that curtain around, dear, so that we might have a scrap of privacy.'

She did as she was asked. 'What's the matter? Are you in any pain that you haven't mentioned?'

'Goodness, no. It's nothing to do with me.'

'I'm sorry. I don't under—'

'It's you and that beau of yours, Mr O'Donnell,' she said in whispered tones. 'I've heard the gossip and don't want to risk even more being spread—that's why I'm whispering.'

Leesa smiled. 'Thank you,' she replied.

'It's not usually my place to meddle but I can't bear to see the two of you at odds with each other—and don't go denying it. Previously, when I've been in having bits of me removed and replaced, you were friends and that was all. Then this last time—when I had my knee arthroscoped—things had changed. I remember saying to Richard how it was about time that nice Mr O'Donnell came to his senses to see what was right in front of him. We were so happy for you both. Now, though, things have become worse. He doesn't stand so close to you any more, he's lost all the sparkle from his smile and constantly avoids meeting your eyes.'

Leesa sighed. 'He's a complex man.'

'Oh, you don't have to tell me that, lovey. I know all about the complex types. My Richard is one of them. We were in a similar situation. Our families had known each other for years and I'd been in love with him since...well, I must have been just a tot. Finally, he came around and we've been together now for nearly fifty years. I wanted you to know that I understand what you're going through. Persistence is the key. Just keep on loving him and you can't go wrong.'

Leesa slowly smiled at the other woman. 'Thank you. It means a lot for you to tell me that. It seems as though I've been in love with him for ever, waiting and planning. Our families have expected for so long that we'd eventually get together.'

'Don't doubt it, dear.'

'It's nice to talk to someone who's been through it—and come out the victor.'

'Yes, I did. Richard has been a wonderful husband, father and now grandfather. After all these years he still loves me as his bride. You know for a fact that your young man will come around.'

'He has to.' Leesa nodded slowly. 'If he doesn't…'

'Don't even think like that. Fight for him—with everything you've got. Use that natural charm of yours. Don't let him off the hook—not even for a second.'

Leesa raised her chin a little, a hint of defiance in her gaze. 'You're right. I've been easing up on him—not wanting to push but not backing off either. I think I *will* just let him have it.'

'That 'a girl.' Mrs Leonard's smile was radiant. The physiotherapist poked her head around the curtain.

'I'll see you later,' Leesa said as she stood. 'And thank you.'

'My pleasure.'

Hamish was pleased with the way his operating list ran that afternoon. Leesa was her usual professional self, and apart from a few of the comments she'd casually dropped about their relationship—or lack of it—she appeared to be handling his exodus quite well.

A surge of big-brotherly pride flooded through him as he walked towards the male changing rooms. She was doing fine. He stopped in his tracks as he saw her talking to Anthony Quinlan, a general surgeon, outside the changing rooms.

She was laughing up at him, her neck exposed in that flirty way she usually did with him. Hamish clenched his hands into fists, telling himself it was merely a big-brother reaction. He forced himself to walk towards them, his legs suddenly feeling like lead.

She laughed at something Anthony had said. 'Sure. I'll meet you there, then.' She smiled at him.

'Great,' Anthony replied. When he saw Hamish coming,

LUCY CLARK   161

he said, 'Catch you then.' He entered the changing rooms, followed by Hamish.

'Hamish.' Anthony nodded, a lock of his blond hair falling across his forehead. He walked off without waiting for an acknowledgment.

Gritting his teeth together, Hamish wrenched his locker door open and took his clothes out. Usually, he'd shower and change, but today he just wanted to get out of the hospital.

When he arrived back at his brother's house he expected to find Leesa there, but Gabby simply shrugged when he asked after her. Charlotte was getting ready for her bath so Hamish spent some time with his niece, having learnt how to get the little rascal clean without her soaking him.

'You're an angel,' he told the sleeping little girl as she snuggled into his arms, almost an hour later. He put her to bed.

'I'm off,' Gabby told him when he returned to the kitchen.

'Where?' he asked with surprise.

'I have a date. I spoke to you and Leesa about it the other morning at breakfast and you said it wouldn't be a problem.'

'So I did. Sorry.' Hamish smiled wearily. 'I'd forgotten.'

'I can cancel.'

'No, go. Have a good time.'

'Thanks. I'll sleep at Mum's tonight as I might be in rather late.'

'Sure. See you tomorrow.'

Leesa still wasn't back. Where was she? It wasn't like her to be this late. He cursed himself for getting worried. She was a grown woman and she was probably trying to prove that she didn't need to answer to him or anyone else.

Deciding to have the shower he'd rejected at the hospital, Hamish took the baby monitor into the bathroom with him. Thankfully, Charlotte seemed to be sleeping soundly and he managed to shower and dress without hearing a peep from her.

He was just returning to the kitchen to find something for dinner when he heard Leesa's car pull up. Without thinking, he stormed outside.

'Where have you been?' he asked, and pointed to his watch. 'It's almost—'

'Eight o'clock,' she finished as she collected bags from her car. 'I had some shopping to do. Why? Is Charlotte all right?'

'She's fine—sleeping soundly.'

'Then what's the problem?' She walked past him and carried the bags to her room. Hamish followed.

'Gabby's not here.'

'I know. She has a date and she'll be staying the night at her mother's house.'

'I expected you to be here.'

'*You* were the one who told Gabby it was no problem if she went out, not me, thereby implying that you'd look after Charlotte.'

'I'd assumed you'd be here, too.'

She turned and smiled sweetly at him. 'Never assume, Hamish.' Leesa pulled a midnight blue piece of cloth from a bag and held it up against her. 'What do you think?'

Hamish relaxed. 'So you're planning on doing a bit of sewing tonight?'

'Yes. I have a date at nine.'

His back became rigid again. 'What?' He spoke the word clearly yet dangerously quietly.

'I have a date,' she repeated as she stood in front of the mirror, manoeuvring the material.

'With Anthony Quinlan,' he stated.

'Yes. I haven't done a bit of sewing for a while and decided on something new for tonight.'

It was a test, Hamish realised. She was making something new and going out on a date with another man, simply to make him jealous. He relaxed again. 'The colour suits you very well. It's similar to that dress you made for Janet's and Angus's wedding anniversary.'

Leesa looked quickly at him. 'I didn't think you'd remember it.'

'I remember a lot of things,' he replied, and walked towards her. He took the material from her hands and forced her to stand still. Slowly, without touching her anywhere else, he bent his head and kissed her once, twice, three times on the lips before she snagged his lower lip between her teeth and deepened the kiss.

In return, she didn't touch him either. Just their lips—and their souls, Hamish realised. He broke away and looked down into her eyes which were clouded with desire.

'Have fun on your date,' he said with a raised eyebrow.

'I will.' She smiled slowly at him and took the material back.

CHAPTER TEN

FORTY-FIVE minutes later, Leesa walked into the lounge room where Hamish was sitting, reading a medical journal. He looked up and she smiled, twirling around for him.

'What do you think?'

He swallowed a few times, before answering, 'I think you're a magician when it comes to a piece of material.'

'Simple yet elegant. Stunning yet sexy.' The light she saw flash in his eyes revealed he wasn't as disinterested as he was letting on. She'd designed the dress for him—not Anthony Quinlan. It had one-inch straps, a low V-neckline, showed off her incredible figure and finished mid-thigh. She collected her keys and checked her handbag, waiting for him to say something more.

'Have a good time. Don't worry about Charlotte. She'll be fine with good old Uncle Hamish.'

'Of course she will be,' Leesa replied, and watched as he turned his attention back to the medical journal, leaving her with the only option of walking out the door. 'Don't wait up,' she couldn't resist calling.

'You look incredible,' Anthony Quinlan said as the *maître d'* at Elizabeth's, seated her opposite him. Elizabeth's was an exclusive restaurant in the heart of Newcastle, and she'd been surprised when Anthony had suggested it.

'Thank you,' she replied with a smile.

'So, how'd things go with Hamish?'

'All right, I guess.' She shrugged. 'Thanks again for your help but I don't think it's working. Hamish just isn't the jealous type.'

'Don't you believe it. I could tell he wanted to rip me

apart in the changing rooms this afternoon. It's working all right.'

The table they sat at was for four. 'Who else is coming?' she asked.

'Augustine Pinkerton…and Jake Tindall. You know Pink, don't you? Of course you do,' he continued, answering his own question. Leesa watched as he fidgeted with his wineglass.

'Yes, I know Pink.' She hesitated for a moment, before asking, 'Is something wrong, Anthony?'

'No.' He looked up at her. 'Why would you think anything was wrong?'

Leesa smiled. 'No reason.'

'Here they come,' he mumbled. 'Uh, just so we're clear, Leesa. You know there's nothing but friendship between the two of us.' His tone was low as he watched Pink, in particular, walk slowly through the restaurant. 'I've agreed to help you make Hamish jealous, but that's it.'

'Exactly,' she answered, before turning to say hello to Jake and Pink. She would think about Anthony's behavior later—right now she was bent on enjoying herself.

During the course of the meal the conversations were lively. They talked about hospital matters as well as other topics. Jake kept them all amused as he recounted his two ex-wives' attempts to outdo each other with their expense accounts.

'Doesn't that bother you?' Anthony asked, his expression a scowl.

'What can I do about it?' Jake asked. 'I pay them both the same amount—' He broke off and looked carefully around the restaurant before whispering, 'But neither of them know this little fact. One always thinks the other gets more.'

'How do you know so much about your ex-wives' expense accounts?' Leesa couldn't resist asking.

'They take great relish in not only calling one another

but calling me as well. That's the main reason I have an answering machine and spend a lot of time at the hospital.'

'So who's wife number three?' Anthony asked, and Jake quickly shook his head.

'Not for me. I'm through with wives.'

They ordered coffee, and not for the first time that evening Leesa noted the way Anthony had his body turned more towards Pink, who was sitting next to him. He'd been sneaking glances at her when he'd thought no one had been looking, and his earlier words about friendship began to make sense.

'Leesa, I have to ask,' Pink said, after spooning sugar into her cup. 'Where's Hamish?'

All three of them looked at her with interest. As they were all good friends, she decided that only the truth would do.

'Hamish is at home, babysitting Charlotte.'

'By himself?' Jake asked. When Leesa nodded, he continued, 'The man has guts. Even though I got married twice, I was never stupid enough to have kids.'

'You don't have to be stupid to have kids,' Pink hotly contradicted.

'That's not what I meant,' Jake clarified. 'Being surrounded by pregnant women all day in Obstetrics is perfect for you, and no doubt you want a gaggle of children—'

'At least six,' Pink interrupted with defiance.

'All I'm saying is that it's not for me.'

Leesa looked at Anthony, who was trying to hide a smile. 'I've always wanted kids,' he put in.

Pink smiled at Anthony, before breaking her gaze away to look at Leesa. 'So, have you and Hamish...how shall I put this?'

'Broken up?' Leesa supplied. 'Hamish thinks we have.'

'But you've yet to tell him otherwise,' Jake added with a laugh. 'Good for you, Leesa.'

'I decided to ask Anthony to help me make Hamish jealous. You know, get him to come to his senses.'

'We can help out as well,' Pink said with a gleam of mischief in her eyes. 'After all, the hospital rumour mill needs rumours and innuendo to help it function properly.'

'Yes,' Jake chimed in. 'We can say you and Anthony were all over each other like a rash.'

'Not necessarily *all over* each other,' Pink interjected. 'Perhaps more like that you really seem interested in one another.'

'That sounds better.' Anthony nodded.

'Thanks.' Leesa smiled at all three of them.

'What are friends for?' Anthony asked rhetorically.

Leesa crept into Janet's house early the next morning. She wore a comfortable pair of jeans with a royal blue top. Her hair was pulled back carelessly in a ponytail and she kicked her shoes off by the back door.

Creeping across to the kitchen, she switched the kettle on to make some coffee.

'Nice of you to return,' Hamish said as he walked into the room, looking dishevelled and unkempt. Stubble had formed on his face and his hair was messy. His chest was bare, a pair of pyjama bottoms riding low on his hips.

Leesa unconsciously licked her lips, marvelling at how incredibly handsome he was. She stared at him for a long moment as he sat down on a bench stool. 'Coffee?' she finally asked, after kick-starting her brain.

'Thanks.' There was another pause before he said, 'I know you said not to wait up for you, but I *had* expected you home at some point.'

'Sorry.' She went through the motions of coffee-making. 'I'd planned to, but in the end I—'

'Decided that Anthony Quinlan was too good to pass up? I'm surprised you let him talk you into staying over after just one date. Where's your common sense?'

Leesa frowned at him. 'Anthony and I have known each other for years—medical school, internships, registrar training.'

'And that's supposed to justify staying out all night with him? You had responsibilities here.'

'To whom? You were with Charlotte. She was being well cared for by her Uncle Hamish.' Leesa flicked on the baby monitor that sat on the bench.

'She's not in her room—she's in mine,' he growled, and she turned the monitor off again.

'So that's your real problem. You had your precious sleep interrupted by Charlotte.'

'That is not my problem,' he argued. 'Charlotte wasn't any bother. Pity I can't say the same for her aunt.'

'Oh, I see—so when you were talking about responsibilities, you meant to *you?*'

When he didn't reply, Leesa shook her head in amazement. 'You have no claim on me, Hamish. You may care for me. You may want me. You may love me—but you're not going to do anything about it.

'You know I love you,' she continued. 'I have for most of my life, but seeing that you've rejected me—*completely*—why on earth do you think I'd wait around here at your beck and call, lapping up the platonic friendship you're offering? I'm sorry, Hamish, but I refuse to beat myself up and wallow in self-pity because the man I love doesn't want me. I'm trying to make a new start. To get on with my life. And if that means dating Anthony Quinlan and staying out all night, then that's what I'll do, and you have absolutely no right whatsoever to dictate otherwise.'

She stormed off to check on Charlotte. 'Think about *that*,' she muttered, and continued praying he'd come to his senses.

After that incident in the kitchen, Leesa hardly saw Hamish for the next few days. On Monday she arranged for

Roxanne Hannover to help him with the operating list while she concentrated on the research project. She heard no complaints from Hamish so she gathered everything had worked out fine.

She visited Mr Lewis in the rehabilitation hospital and was pleased with his progress. Mrs Leonard was also progressing well, and on Thursday afternoon was transferred to the rehabilitation hospital. Leesa went with her and, after seeing her settled in, then drove to the airport to meet the parents.

Not surprisingly, Hamish was there as well, and while they waited for their parents to come through customs Hamish sat down beside her.

'Truce?' he asked, and held out his hand.

'Why?'

'I don't think it's necessary to bring our parents into the—'

'Feud?' she supplied, and he shrugged.

'Feud between us.'

'Do you think they're completely unobservant? They'll know within seconds that things aren't right between us. You've taken responsibility for everyone else during your life, Hamish, but now you need to take responsibility for yourself. Your actions, your pride, your stubbornness and your reserve are just some of the traits stopping us from being ecstatically happy. I'm sorry. No truce.'

Carol Stevenson was pushing her luggage trolley towards them and Leesa rushed over to greet her mother.

The next few hours were a mixture of talking, laughing and excitement as they all returned to Janet's and Angus's house. Charlotte was embraced but not stifled by all four grandparents.

'She needs time to get to know us,' Mary O'Donnell reasoned, and relinquished her to Gabby's care. 'How are Janet and Angus? Ready to come home tomorrow?'

'The reports from their surgeons are very good, but personally I think they've both been ready for ages to return home,' Leesa replied.

'Let's go and see them.' Sean O'Donnell picked up Hamish's car keys. 'Mind if I drive, son?'

'Yes, why don't you, Hamish, Carol and Ron go in Hamish's car, and Leesa and I will go in her car?' Mary organised. 'We'll leave Gabby to put Charlotte to bed in peace.'

There was no disputing Mary O'Donnell once she'd set her mind to something, and everyone complied. Hamish hesitated only slightly before his mother shooed him away.

'What's the status between you and Hamish?' Mary asked as Leesa backed out of the driveway.

'He's completely rejected me,' Leesa replied matter-of-factly.

'He loves you.'

'I know. He told me so himself.'

Mary was stunned for a moment. 'He's admitted to loving you?'

'Yes.'

'Then what's the problem? No, don't tell me,' she continued. 'Let me think.'

Leesa continued to drive towards the hospital, feeling completely relaxed in Mary's company.

'He's afraid to marry again,' Mary declared triumphantly a few minutes later. 'I'm right, aren't I?'

'Spot on.'

'So what are you doing about it?'

'I'm helping him come to his senses by making him insanely jealous.'

'Is it working?'

'Slowly. Give him another few weeks and everything should be organised.'

'He said you have a conference overseas at the end of June. It's now the end of March. Any chance we can organise a wedding before you leave?'

Leesa pulled into the doctors' car park and turned to smile at her soon-to-be mother-in-law. 'I don't see why not.'

Mary laughed as she climbed out of the car. 'Look at his face,' she remarked quietly to Leesa as they watched Hamish walk towards them. 'He's worried sick at what we've been scheming.'

'He has every right to be,' Leesa replied with a sweet smile.

'Everything…all right?' he asked, looking from his mother then to Leesa and back again.

'Why wouldn't it be, darling?' Mary asked as she looped her hand through his arm. 'Daughters-in-law are such precious people,' Mary chattered as they walked through the car park and into the hospital.

'Pardon?' Hamish said quickly, and glanced at Leesa, a concerned look on his face.

'Janet,' Mary clarified. 'You all know that I love her and Leesa as my surrogate daughters, but I confess that when we learned of Janet's feelings for Angus, and I realised she would become my legal daughter-in-law, I was so happy.'

'That's—nice, Mum,' Hamish said hesitantly, and ran a finger around his shirt collar. Leesa tried hard not to smile and kept her gaze focused on the ground as Mary continued.

'It's a real shame you and Leesa won't follow their example.'

'*What?*' Hamish demanded, and tried to stop walking, but Mary tugged him along.

'Don't stop. I'm impatient to see Angus and Janet. Leesa told me about her new boyfriend during the ride here. Pity it didn't work out between you two but, then, I guess a mother can't have *everything* she wants. So long as both you and Leesa are happy, that's all that really matters, I suppose.'

When they entered the hospital Mary turned her remarks

to general topics, but Leesa could tell Hamish was still in shock from his mother's words.

They spent an hour at the hospital before the travellers complained of tiredness.

'We're so glad you're both feeling better,' Carol said as she kissed her son-in-law and daughter goodbye.

'*We're* looking forward to coming home tomorrow,' Janet replied. 'The last four weeks haven't been the best we've ever shared.'

'Once you're both home,' Leesa said, 'I'm sure your recovery rate will increase. It's amazing how familiar surroundings can help a person recuperate. The district nurse will be around every day to check your dressings and pin sites—that sort of thing—and then you'll have Hamish and me dropping in regularly to give you both a thorough check-up.'

'And you'll have your parents and your in-laws there to help you, care for you and generally drive you around the twist,' Sean O'Donnell put in.

'It sounds worse than being in here,' Angus complained with a grin.

'Come on. It's time we all went home,' Mary ordered. 'Carol, why don't you and I ride back with Leesa this time?'

'Sounds good.' Carol nodded.

In the car Mary broke the news to Carol about Leesa's and Hamish's wedding. 'We'll pick up the paperwork tomorrow.' She clapped her hands excitedly.

'Hamish will resent this,' Carol said with a smile on her face. 'He'll say we're trying to control his life.'

'Someone has to,' Mary retorted. 'I'll take any blame. He can never stay mad at me for long. After all, I endured a long and painful labour—to bring him into the world. As far as I'm concerned, that gives me a licence to meddle in his life, especially when he's too blind and stubborn to see what's right before his eyes.' She gestured to Leesa who was just listening to the other women with interest.

If Hamish had thought she was bad when it came to scheming, it was nothing compared to their mothers.

One week later, after Hamish and Leesa had returned to their own apartments, the entire family met again at Janet's and Angus's house to celebrate Charlotte's first birthday. It was the Thursday before the Easter long weekend so both Leesa and Hamish were hard pressed to leave the hospital on time.

Leesa was glad she'd made it as the doting grandparents had spared no expense. The house was filled with streamers and balloons. Brightly coloured, wrapped presents awaited the little girl, who simply adored being the centre of attention. Cameras flashed and video cameras whirled as the event was captured for ever.

'It took us a long time to choose exactly the right cake,' Mary announced as they took the cake out of the box. 'I know Janet would have loved to have made her daughter's first birthday cake, but she's still not completely recovered.'

'She was disappointed,' Carol added, 'but there'll be other years and other children.'

'Are you talking about me again?' Janet asked as she hobbled into the room and slumped thankfully down onto the bench stool.

'Just talking about the cake, dear.' Mary nodded and set the birthday cake out.

'I would have loved to have made her one, but...' Janet trailed off as she admired the Winnie-the-Pooh cake Mary was setting out. 'It's a great cake,' she added with enthusiasm.

'Turn out the lights,' Carol called through to the dining room as Janet lit the one candle in the centre of the cake. A hush settled over the family as they waited for the cake.

In the stillness, Hamish's beeper sounded and he quickly switched it off.

'Happy birthday to you,' they all began to sing as Mary carried the cake into the dining room. Charlotte watched with delight and clapped her hands a few times. When it was time for her to blow out the candle, her father helped her, even though Grandma Carol had been coaching her all week long in the art of blowing.

When the lights were switched on again, Leesa's pager sounded. She looked across at Hamish and they both shrugged.

'At least have a piece of cake before you go,' Mary insisted.

They both rang the hospital, before quickly eating a piece of cake and kissing their niece goodnight.

'Looks as though the long weekend has begun with a vengeance,' Hamish remarked as they walked out to their cars.

'One motor vehicle accident after another. Isn't that the way the weekend works?'

'You're becoming more cynical,' he observed as he waited for her to unlock her car. He held the door open for her.

'Must be the company I'm keeping,' she answered. During the past week she and Anthony had been out on two dates. The hospital grapevine was well and truly buzzing.

Leesa was surprised when Hamish reached for her, bringing his lips to meet hers in a hard and punishing kiss. She met him evenly, wanting to punish him in return, but soon their mutual need for each other won out and the kiss became filled with desire and passion.

'He's not right for you,' Hamish growled when his lips finally broke from hers, their breathing ragged and uneven.

'Who is?'

'Pardon?'

'Who is right for me, Hamish?' Leesa looked eagerly up

into his eyes, seeing the answer there and hoping he'd say it out loud. His gaze dropped to her mouth for a fleeting moment before he stepped away.

Her anger returned at his withdrawal. 'See you in Theatre,' she snapped as she climbed into the car and slammed the door.

Three weeks later the hospital grapevine had stopped buzzing regarding the relationship between Leesa and Anthony and had accepted them as a couple. When both of them were free, which usually turned out to be once or twice a week, they'd have dinner together at one of the many restaurants close to the hospital.

Sometimes they went with other colleagues and other times it was just the two of them. Leesa really enjoyed Anthony's company and it was actually helping to keep her mind off Hamish, but when she returned to her lonely and empty apartment the longings for the man she truly loved would return and encompass her.

'Are you free this Saturday?' Mary called to ask her one evening. 'Carol and I want to start looking at material for the wedding dresses.'

'Then the planning is coming along just fine?'

'Just as we've discussed.'

'It's a pity the groom doesn't know about it.' Her voice held sadness and longing.

'He'll be there. You're not on emergency call, are you?'

'No. I have a few hours free. I'm going out with Anthony and need to make a new dress.'

'Tell me again you're not serious about this Anthony person?' Mary asked directly.

'Mary, I've been in love with your son for an eternity. Anthony is just a friend who's helping Hamish come to his senses. He's more than happy to keep our relationship platonic.'

'Well, it's working beautifully. Hamish was here last

night, moping around. None of us have ever seen him like this before. He's pining for you.'

Leesa sighed. 'Am I doing the right thing? Perhaps I should go over and—'

'Don't you dare. Your plan is working brilliantly. Hamish needs to come to the realisation that you're the one and only person for him—all by himself. He's too stubborn to listen to anyone else, otherwise you'd have been married years ago. Now, where are you going that you need a new dress?'

'Accident and Emergency are having their annual Christmas dinner. Most of the hospital's been invited.'

'But it's the end of April.'

'It's about the only time of the year when they're not completely frantic.'

'Will Hamish be going?'

'He wasn't going to go but I managed to change his mind for him.'

'What happened?' Mary asked eagerly.

'One of my friends, Augustine Pinkerton—Pink, we call her—has a thing for Anthony. I'm pretty sure Anthony has a thing for her but neither of them want to make the first move. When I had lunch with Pink the other day, I asked her straight out if she liked him. She said yes. So I suggested she ask Hamish to the dinner, telling him she wanted to make Anthony jealous. This way, he'll definitely come with the hope of consoling me when Pink runs off with Anthony who has just broken my heart.'

'I'm so proud of you.' Mary's voice was filled with happiness.

'That's why my dress needs to be an absolute knockout.'

'Where's the dinner being held?'

'Giovanni's,' Leesa said with a giggle.

'The same restaurant where Angus proposed to Janet?'

'The very same. As far as I know, neither of us have

been there since that night, so those memories will be uppermost in our minds.'

'We'll leave the wedding dresses until later. We *must* make sure you look incredible on Saturday night!'

Hamish offered Pink his arm and the two walked from the car park into the restaurant. There was a line at the door as people's invitations were checked. The hospital had booked the entire restaurant, and when they finally entered the room's festive atmosphere became contagious. Tinsel, lights and a large Christmas tree in the corner of the room ensured that everyone knew this was a Christmas party.

'There they are,' Pink whispered to Hamish, and he looked to where she gestured. When his gaze fell on Leesa he felt a heavy blow to his solar plexus. She was dressed in a strapless black dress that fitted her like a second skin. Her blonde hair was arranged on top of her head, with a few loose tendrils caressing her neck. A choker-chain of diamonds, which he instantly recognised as his mother's, was the only jewellery she wore.

He slowly exhaled as he felt his heart rate begin to increase at the mere sight of her. Pink led the way over, tugging impatiently at his hand. He watched as Quinlan came up behind Leesa and leaned down to whisper something in her ear. She turned her head to look at him, their lips almost touching, before she smiled.

The way she was looking at Quinlan made Hamish sick. He clenched his teeth, fighting hard to resist the urge to slam his fist right into Quinlan's pretty-boy face. She shouldn't be with him. He was no good.

She should be with...*himself.*

'Hi, everyone,' Pink was saying as they finally made it over to the table where Leesa, Quinlan and a few others had congregated.

Hamish merely nodded at everyone, his gaze returning instantly to Leesa. 'You look...good.'

She smiled sweetly at him. 'I think we need to work on your vocabulary, Hamish, but "good" will do for now.'

'Leesa, I *love* your dress,' Pink was saying. 'Don't make me envious by admitting you made it.'

'Leesa makes most of her own clothes,' Hamish remarked. 'She always has.'

'Sorry, Pink, but Hamish is right. I made it.'

'No wonder it fits you so perfectly. Twirl around for me,' Pink instructed.

Hamish watched Leesa as she twirled for her friend. It did fit her perfectly.

'That choker is stunning.' Pink leaned forward for a closer look. 'Are they real diamonds?'

'Yes,' Hamish replied once again. Pink turned to him for clarification. 'It's my mother's necklace.'

'Hamish's father gave it to her on the night he proposed.' Leesa looked up at Anthony and smiled. He smiled back and she returned her attention to Pink. 'It had belonged to his mother so it's been a family heirloom for generations. I couldn't believe it when Mary suggested I wear it tonight, but it does go perfectly with the dress.'

She risked a glance at Hamish to find his expression one of sheer shock. Good. Her plan was working perfectly. Leesa and Anthony had had a long discussion prior to their arrival. She'd told him that tonight would be their last date together, even if Hamish didn't come to his senses. She'd also told him to let the night unfold and not to worry about her.

'What do you mean by that?' Anthony had asked.

'Pink is coming as Hamish's date.'

'I didn't think she was coming.' His eyes had lit up with delight.

'So you do have feelings for her?'

'Am I that obvious?'

'Not to her,' Leesa had remarked. 'As I said, just let the night unfold and don't worry about me.'

She'd also rearranged some of the seating when they'd arrived at Giovanni's. Pink and Anthony were sitting next to each other and Hamish was next to her, across the table from their dates.

Dinner was a lavish affair with all the trimmings. Turkey, ham, beef with lots of vegetables and Christmas pudding for dessert.

Anthony literally took Leesa at her words and paid her little attention, preferring to let Pink know that he was definitely interested. As this was exactly what Pink wanted, she in turn paid Hamish little attention, leaving the two family friends safely in each other's company.

'Do you remember the last time we were here?' Hamish asked her softly as he sipped his wine.

'Angus's and Janet's engagement.' She looked up at him and their gazes locked.

'Would you care to step outside for some air?' Hamish asked, and Leesa nodded, collecting her bag.

They walked around to the side of the restaurant where there was a little pond and a park bench. Leesa shivered slightly and Hamish quickly took off his jacket and placed it around her shoulders.

'I hope you're not too upset about Quinlan. I'm furious with the way he's been neglecting you all night long.'

Leesa shook her head as she sat down. 'I'm not…too upset.'

He watched her for a long moment. 'No, in fact, you appear to have expected him to neglect you.'

'I knew Pink liked him and he liked her. I guess it was only a matter of time before they realised it. Anthony and I are just friends, Hamish. Strictly platonic,' she added with emphasis. She didn't want Hamish to think there was anything serious between her and the blond surgeon.

'That's not the way it looked when I walked in tonight. You were smiling up at him like a Cheshire cat.'

'Jealous, Hamish?'

'Yes. All right, I admit it. I was jealous.' The words were ground out furiously, as though he hated himself for admitting to such a weakness.

'And *why* were you jealous?'

'Because you belong with me.' He raked a hand through his hair.

Leesa sighed with happiness. 'It's about time you realised it.'

He was silent for a while, before sitting down beside her. 'I'm beginning to think I've been expertly manipulated.'

'You don't appear to mind too much.'

He took her hand in his. 'I can't believe you know me so well.'

'Believe it, my darling,' she whispered, and placed a kiss on his lips. 'Accept it.' She kissed him again. 'Embrace it.'

This time when her lips touched his he didn't let her go. Wrapping his arms around her shoulders, he drew her closer. His mouth moved over hers in a soft, sensual and serious way. His lips were tender and loving and Leesa felt warmed right throughout her being.

'You know I love you, Leesa.'

'I love you, too.' She smiled contentedly, before snuggling against him and resting her head on his chest.

'I feel so…unprepared.'

'For what?'

'To propose to you. Angus proposed to Janet with such flamboyance and presented her not only with a coffee-pot but with a beautiful engagement ring. My father had this beautiful necklace to present to my mother when he proposed all those years ago. Yet here I am, knowing that if I let you out of my grasp for even a nanosecond I might lose you for ever.'

Leesa raised her head and looked at him. 'Is marriage to me what you *really* want, Hamish?'

'Not only marriage, Leesa. I want to spend the rest of my life with you. Buying a house of our own, giving

Charlotte some cousins to play with, growing old with you. And I don't care who knows it. The hospital grapevine can buzz all it likes. I love you and I want to be with you.'

She snuggled back against him. 'That's what I want, too.'

'I'm mad at myself for not realising it sooner, otherwise I would have been prepared and my proposal would have been perfect and romantic. Just what you deserve.'

'What makes you think I'm letting you off the hook?' She giggled. 'I may yet demand a romantic proposal from you, Hamish O'Donnell.'

'When I walked in here tonight and saw Quinlan all over you I knew *then* that you belonged with *me*. No one else, Leesa. *Me!*'

'Yes, I do.'

He was silent for a while before saying, 'I've tried so hard for so long to do the right thing where you were concerned.'

'I know. It nearly drove me insane.'

He chuckled. 'Do you remember in your second year of medical school you came to stay at my parents' house for your vacation?'

'I remember. That's when my infatuation for you started to turn serious. You were quite cool towards me at times.'

'I had to be. That was when I realised I wanted you. You were so innocent, so giving, so incredibly sexy and beautiful. I found it difficult to keep my hands off you. You were just starting out on such a wonderful adventure and the last thing you needed was a romantic involvement.

'You wanted to achieve—you'd told me so yourself and you weren't going to let anything stand in your way. You wanted to become an orthopaedic surgeon and I knew you had at least another ten or eleven years of study and training ahead of you. I knew it would be wrong for us to get involved. It would have caused too many complications…so I backed away.

'I schooled my thoughts. I was determined to conquer the burning need I felt every time you walked into the room. I even stood outside your bedroom door a few times, with my hand on the doorknob, knowing that if I entered you wouldn't push me away. It was up to me to be strong for both of us.'

'My knight in shining armour.' Leesa pressed a kiss to his lips. 'Thank you for being strong for both of us. I agree, the timing back then would have been all wrong.'

'You needed to experience life. To achieve your goals. Don't think I didn't see you change over the years. You matured all too quickly for my liking—because it just made it more difficult for me to push you away. I urged you to study, mentored you. It allowed me the opportunity to be close to you in a non-physical relationship. Our minds connected and that helped me through the years, as my attraction for you deepened and grew into the true and faithful love I now feel for you.'

Leesa sat up and took his hand. 'Have you looked up the definition of romance? Because, let me tell you, *this* is romance, Hamish. Professing your emotions, making me feel so loved and special.'

He smiled. 'You are. So loved and so special to me, Leesa.' He kissed her again. 'I've been such a fool, yet you continued to love me. Persevered when most would have given up. A few years before your sister's wedding, you began dating seriously. You have no idea how tortured I was over the fact that you might actually marry one of those losers. Thankfully, you didn't seem to be too serious about any of them but, still, I could have lost you completely. If so, it would have been my own fault.

'At your sister's wedding, I thought I'd ruined it all. I told you how much I desired you, how incredibly sexy you were, but that it couldn't work between us. I do regard you as family, Leesa. *My* family. But again the timing was wrong. I nearly lost your friendship and as that was the only aspect of a relationship I could allow myself to have with you it almost broke me. You withdrew and I hoped and prayed you'd come back to me—and you did.'

'I could never stay mad at you, Hamish. I'd hoped to make you jealous by dating other men. I'd hoped to bring you to your senses by going away for a few years. Nothing seemed to work.'

'I knew you were trying to make me jealous with Quinlan and I was determined to fight it, but as the weeks passed and you still continued to see him I began to think it just might be serious. It scared me. I couldn't sleep properly or think straight. It drove me insane—more so than all those years ago—because this time I'd at least admitted to myself that I loved you.'

'I'm sorry, Hamish, but I felt you were being a little selfish, saying you wouldn't marry me because of your bad experience with Sandra. I had to help you come to your senses.'

'It was a gamble,' he replied.

'It was a calculated risk,' she amended. 'And one with very good odds. We were meant for each other.'

'You've known it all along, my darling Leesa. I was so determined to protect you from myself that I let my own prejudices get in the way. Finally I'm seeing you for who you are. A strong, vibrant and passionate woman. Truly the most perfect woman—for me.'

He stood, before going down on one knee, her hands clasped within his.

'Leesa—I love you. Please, marry me?'

Leesa pretended to consider his words for a second, before saying, 'OK.'

He stood and tugged her to her feet. Wrapping his arms around her, they sealed their union with a passionate and seemingly never-ending kiss.

'Come on,' he said finally, the arm around her shoulders forcing her to move.

'Where are we going?'

'To tell our families the good news.'

'There's no hurry.'

He stopped. 'What does that mean?'

'Just that they're all…well, you know, expecting—'

'The conspiracy has been at work again.' He touched a hand to the choker around her neck for confirmation.

'It's only because we all love you—me most of all.'

Hamish smiled and relaxed, drawing her close to him. 'Care to have a little bit of fun with them?'

Leesa's eyes widened with surprise. 'Hamish! I didn't know you had it in you.'

'So there *are* some things about me you *don't* know.'

'Obviously,' she said, her eyes alive with delight as she pressed her body hard against his. 'Now I'm looking forward to discovering exactly what they are!'

EPILOGUE

'IT WAS a great wedding,' Hamish told his wife as they lay in bed.

'The best,' Leesa agreed, and kissed her husband. When he tried to pull away she deepened the kiss. Reluctantly he broke free.

'Don't start, Mrs O'Donnell. We have a plane to catch.'

They'd driven from Newcastle to Sydney yesterday—the day after their wedding—and were due to fly out to America for the big orthopaedic conference later that morning.

'Spending my honeymoon surrounded by several hundred orthopaedic surgeons wasn't exactly how I'd envisioned it.' Leesa flicked the bedcovers back and stood, languorously stretching. Hamish's gaze devoured her beautiful naked body and when she noticed the desire that filled his eyes she simply flicked her hair over her shoulders and walked to the bathroom.

'Don't start, Mr O'Donnell,' she said, mimicking his words. 'We have a plane to catch.'

She started the shower and wasn't surprised when he appeared in the bathroom. Hamish was everything she'd ever dreamed of in a husband, and as they'd only been husband and wife for two days she still had a lot more to learn.

'I still marvel at how quickly our mothers were able to organise our wedding, even if they *had* been planning it for years. Mum had all the paperwork there, ready to sign the instant they saw the engagement ring on your finger.'

'That was a good idea of yours,' she added as the spray washed over her body. 'Testing their powers of observation. It took a whole two hours before your mother saw the engagement ring.'

'I know. My ears are still ringing from the impact of her squeal. Still, they had the wedding dresses made within a few days, the church had been booked, the flowers organised.'

'Hamish, perhaps there are some things that you're better off not knowing.'

He opened the shower door. 'Such as?'

'The conspiracy. From the instant your parents returned from Egypt, our mothers were actively planning our wedding.'

'You even had the date chosen?'

'Yes. Since we were already due to go overseas to the conference, I thought it a great opportunity to pop across to Cannes for a *real* honeymoon.'

Hamish closed the shower door behind them and reached for the soap. 'How long has the honeymoon suite at the Carlton Hotel, Cannes been booked for?'

'Do you *really* want to know?'

'Not really.' He grinned, before kissing his wife.

MILLS & BOON®

Makes any time special™

Mills & Boon publish 29 new titles every month. Select from...

Modern Romance™   **Tender Romance**™

Sensual Romance™

Medical Romance™   **Historical Romance**™

MAT2

MILLS & BOON®

Medical Romance™

GIVE ME FOREVER by *Caroline Anderson*

Mac's return home takes an unexpected turn when he
discovers that nurse Ruth Walker has returned at the
same time. Once teenage friends, it seems their feelings
have changed with a passion…

LISA'S CHRISTMAS ASSIGNMENT by *Jessica Matthews*

Lisa had kept her distance from Dr Simon Travers until
asked by colleagues to find him a Christmas gift. Now
she was forced to get to know him better…

A REAL FAMILY CHRISTMAS by *Jennifer Taylor*

Nurse Emma Graham had been brought up in a
children's home and had never had a real family
Christmas—so when Dr Daniel Hutton asked her to
join him and his orphaned niece for the day, she readily
agreed.

On sale 1 December 2000